PENGUIN BOOKS
1974
ON THE LOOSE
JOHN STROUD

On the Loose

JOHN STROUD

PENGUIN BOOKS

Penguin Books Ltd, Harmondsworth, Middlesex
AUSTRALIA: Penguin Books Pty Ltd, 762 Whitehorse Road,
Mitcham, Victoria

—

First published by Longmans 1961
Published in Penguin Books 1963

—

Copyright © John Stroud, 1961

—

Made and printed in Great Britain
by Hazell Watson & Viney Ltd
Aylesbury and Slough
Set in Linotype Pilgrim

TO
EILEEN EDWARDS
WITH LOVE

I

THE gears clanged together, there was a shrill cheer from the boys, and the coach lumbered out of the forecourt and down the drive, bouncing ponderously as it hit the pot-holes. The six ugly little boys on the back seat grinned out of the window, their faces like a line of masks hung on a string. The first six to get aboard always hurtled straight into the back, where they played the fool.

The headmaster stood by the steps outside the front door and watched the coach out of sight, not waving, but holding one arm up straight above his head. There were crinkles round his eyes – he thought he felt quite fond of the noisy crew as they disappeared; but it was wearily, almost bitterly, that he re-entered the school. The end of the summer term, the end of the long school year, did not make him feel glad, regretful, or relaxed; his predominant feeling was that he was both old and unsuccessful. The months ahead would be very wearing financially, there was at least one new staff-member to engage, and the paint was peeling in the dining-room. . . .

His wife came across the hall and dumped an armful of grubby sheets in the laundry basket. 'That's that, then,' she said. 'Alone at last!'

The headmaster nodded in silence. He didn't like her very much.

'Morton's left his blazer,' she said, 'and Henry seems to have forgotten to wear any underclothes. And what on earth are we to do with Dumbleton's rabbit? It's still in its hutch.'

'Oh, curse the boy!' muttered the headmaster. 'We shall have to have a *No Pets* rule. I can't wet-nurse the confounded thing. Tell George to kill it and eat it.'

'You can't, Bill! Dumbleton will probably ring up this evening and ask for it.'

'Oh —' His high bald dome was wrinkled with perplexity; the rabbit, at this leaden moment, presented a tiresome problem. 'Let George take it down to the cottage and look after it. Are you making any tea?'

'Yes, the kettle's on. Go and put your feet up for half an hour and read the paper; I'll bring your tea in to you. You can relax for a bit now they're all off the premises.'

'All right; then I'll do that wretched condemning.' He moved across the hall and in the corridor said: 'Oh, damn, Joyce, what's this, here's all Beedman's stuff.'

His wife turned back from the kitchen and gazed helplessly at the suitcase and mac and paper bags. 'Beedman? Has he forgotten his things? Surely he can't have forgotten everything.'

'Has he gone?'

'He must have done, his father was coming before lunch.'

'Did you see him?'

'No, I thought you had.'

'I haven't seen him.' The headmaster felt utterly despondent. 'What the devil's the matter with the man? I can't pack this rubbish up and send it through the post.'

'Perhaps Beedman's still here.'

The headmaster gazed at her sullenly. Was there no end to his responsibilities?

'Beedman!' he barked. He went back into the hall and hurled his voice up the stairs. '*Beedman!*'

Far down at the end of the corridor behind him a door opened, emitting a shaft of light. A small figure trudged slowly along, emerged into the hall and stood blinking at them.

'Yes, sir?'

The headmaster stared at him crossly. 'Haven't you gone, Beedman?'

'No, sir.'

'Your father was supposed to be here before lunch!'

'Yes, sir.'

'Had you better ring them up, Bill?' asked his wife.

'Where do you live, Beedman?'

'Francombe, sir.'

The call would cost at least 1s. 6d. The headmaster stared at the boy moodily. Then he glanced at his watch. 'I'll give your father another half-hour, then I'll have to telephone. What are you doing?'

'Reading, sir.'

'Well, you'd better – oh, all right, go on reading.'

Half an hour with his feet up now seemed highly desirable to the headmaster. He dragged himself into the study and sat down. Then he began to fidget. How the hell could he deal with this intrusive boy? Francombe was across country and the rail journey would mean at least two changes; he could hardly send the boy unaccompanied. The bus route was no better. So long as Beedman remained on the premises the headmaster felt insecure and uneasy. After twenty minutes he began walking to and fro irresolutely. Then he picked up the phone, obtained the Francombe number from Directory Enquiries and got himself put through.

A woman's voice answered. 'I'm afraid I don't understand,' she said. 'My husband left here this morning to drive down and fetch the boy. I really can't help you : I have a visitor.'

'All the boys have left here except little Royston,' said the headmaster, trying to be silky because the Beedmans paid the fees regularly.

'You mean you're afraid of being saddled with him?'

'Oh, no, no, not that; I wondered if there had possibly been a change of plan?'

'No,' said Mrs Beedman. 'Gilbert was going to see some people down your way somewhere; I expect he's been hung up.'

'If there has been an accident –' suggested the headmaster delicately.

'Oh, no, I'd have heard by now. Gilbert'll be along. Or can't you put the boy on the train?'

'I'd much prefer you to come over and –'

'Couldn't possibly,' she said. 'Look here, I must go. Ring me in half an hour and tell me what's happening, yes? Goodbye.'

'Could I beg you to –'

But she had quickly rung off.

The headmaster replaced his own phone and gazed glumly

at it. His shoes were beginning to feel too small. He went down and got the boy to help with sorting out text-books. The half-hour dragged past. The headmaster felt reluctant to spend more money on telephone calls about the wretched boy who was working so silently beside him; it was a relief when the phone rang and Mrs Beedman came through.

'Hasn't Gilbert got there yet? What the hell's the man playing at? Can't Royston come by train, for God's sake? He's old enough.'

'There isn't a train now till eight tonight.'

'Oh, God. I'll have to come down. Look here, if Gilbert turns up, will you tell him I've got Sheila's car and I'm on my way. Have you got that?'

'Yes.'

'Damn it. I'll be there in two hours.'

Twenty minutes later there was an echoing blare on a horn, the gravel scrunched and a scarlet car came to a plunging halt outside. Gilbert Beedman didn't climb out, but waited for them to come running. He was a short, stout man with a round bald spot and the habit of carrying his head flung back, his jaw jutting.

'Hallo, Dunnet.'

'Good afternoon, Mr Beedman. We were getting quite worried about you, as you said you would come at –'

'I know. Had an appointment at eleven with some fellers at Larchfield and they kept me on for lunch there, you know how it is. How are you?'

'Pretty fair. And you?'

'Can't grumble.'

'Your wife telephoned.' And the headmaster gave the message.

'Now what the hell does she want to do that for? She knew I was coming. Put your stuff in the boot, Royston. Oh my God, what a stupid thing!'

The headmaster was silent, stooping awkwardly by the car window and looking at his shoes. Royston closed the boot and stood uncertainly on the other side of the car.

'I'll keep a look-out for her on the way back, that's all I can do,' said Mr Beedman, drumming his stubby fingers impatiently on the steering wheel. 'If she turns up, tell her I've gone on, will you? Ridiculous nonsense, fussing over nothing. How's this one?'

The headmaster glanced covertly at Royston and said: 'Oh, pretty fair. Making progress.'

'Got rid of those moods yet?'

'He does have his moods at times,' admitted the headmaster.

'Huh. Flipping family I've got. Get in, Royston, we must be off.'

The boy sidled into his seat and closed the door, too gently: his father leant across and slammed it. 'That's it, well – look after yourself, Dunnet.'

'And yourself, Mr Beedman. Good-bye, Royston.'

The boy nodded without shifting his glance from the windscreen. Then the car started and spurted over the gravel. The headmaster watched them out of sight, raising his arm once in farewell; he felt relief and also an ironic amusement over the ill-matched pair and when they were gone he shook his head and quirked his mouth resignedly. Then depression settled on him again and he trudged back to the chores of clearing up and to his wife.

Mr Beedman drove fiercely down the drive, cursing under his breath at every pot-hole, and swept on to the main road in a flurry of small stones. For some miles he drove in silence, swirling contemptuously past an L-driver on a narrow bend. After they got on to the trunk road he seemed to relax and lit a cigarette. He smelt faintly of whisky and brilliantine. Presently he said: 'So you still get in these moods, eh?'

The boy was silent.

'What do you do, throw things about? Why the hell don't you grow up?' Royston gave an almost imperceptible shrug but remained silent.

'You'll have to pull your finger out if you want to get anywhere, my lad.' Twelve years old and behaving like a great baby.'

Mr Beedman's foot slackened a little on the accelerator, but they were still doing over sixty. 'What's the school like?' he asked.

This time Royston's shrug was more pronounced. 'All right,' he said.

'So it damn well ought to be, at the price I'm paying for it. You're bloody well going to be worth it, I'll tell you now.'

Royston held his peace, and his father began to hum some sort of march. They went round Moleford in silence and Mr Beedman said: 'Have to keep a watch-out for your mother, I suppose. What's the number of Mrs Maxted's car?'

'TJH 734,' said Royston automatically.

'A Minor?'

'Yes.'

'Fat chance we've got of seeing her in all this lot.' It was around rush-hour time and traffic was quite heavy. 'Of all the chronic things to do. Your mother wants her head testing.'

Mr Beedman's fingers began to drum again and the speed of the car increased. They covered a good many miles in silence before a pretty piece of cutting-in on a round-about brought a little relaxation. Mr Beedman had another cigarette. 'Why didn't you go to camp with the Scouts?' he asked.

Royston considered and said: 'Didn't like the idea.'

'You'd have had a good time. Toughened you up, made a man of you. I was a Scout.'

Presently he added: 'I can't get away this summer. I suppose your mother'll take you out somewhere.'

They had seen nothing of Mrs Beedman and they were nearly home.

'I don't mind what you do, so long as you keep out of trouble.'

They came into the Old Town and turned left by the road-house. Shops were crowded thickly together up this road, shuttered now; here and there was a café with its lights ablaze. Knots of long-legged youths were beginning to assemble on their bikes in the gutters, and girls joined them and teetered about on the edge of the pavement. Mr Beedman went past them without noticing, and was doing forty-five over the level crossing and up into the chestnut-shadowed avenues of the New Town. But he slowed circumspectly for the tight turn into his own drive and the crunching rumble down to the garage. Then he turned off the engine, and stretched his arm flamboyantly to look at his watch. 'That's not bad! Hour and three-quarters door to door, *and* through the rush. Out you hop, Samson.'

Royston obediently unloaded his things from the boot and held the garage door open while the car rolled in. Mr Beedman was quite jovial; he hurried from the garage with an air of satisfaction in a job well done and thwacked Royston playfully on the bottom with his paper. 'You go to camp next year and I'll buy you a bike, there you are,' he said, and strutted into the house, only to stop dead when he surveyed the dining-room.

'Bloody hell-fire!' he snarled. 'She hasn't even bothered to leave the tea ready!'

The summer holidays had begun.

2

ROYSTON moved very slowly through the nettles, balancing on one foot while he stretched forward with the other, making sure that when he brought his weight forward his foot would go down cleanly on a crushed bunch of nettles and he would not get stung. He was nearly out, and there was a trail through the tall stingers behind him. Up here at the top end of the field was a wide belt of nettles stretching up to the hedge, which was overgrown and hung down in great thorny sprays. The middle of the hedge seemed to be hollow, as though a series of big caves had been gouged out of the thorn. It was a very hot and silent afternoon; if he had listened, he could have heard the traffic roaring through the Old Town, but at the moment he had the sensation that he was a tiny ant moving under an immense and silent bowl. So silent was it that he could feel God's great eyes boring into his back. He took another step forward.

He wanted to get in under the hedge and have a look round: he thought there might be a body in there. Well, there might very well be, for it was very dark and silent. Now he had come to the ticklish bit, where the last of the nettles were around his feet but the first of the thorns hung down in front of his eyes. Cautiously he trod back the nettles until he could stoop and wriggle in on to the bare moist earth under the hedge. He squatted there motionless for some time, his heart beginning to thump. It was a queer dark place; its secrecy seemed menacing and the earth under his fingers was like a dry sponge, unnatural somehow. He began to creep unwillingly forward, not daring to turn his head to glance at the sunlit meadow behind him. He thought he would see a naked foot first – that or an outflung hand. Wasn't that knobby thing a–suddenly a twig cracked loudly and a bird hurtled through the leaves just over his head. Royston froze; his forehead felt icy, his heart was thudding violently.

He stayed there, crouched close to the earth, not moving a muscle, for a long time. Then, with infinite caution, he stretched one leg backward and started to retreat on all fours. He began to feel that this dark place was alive and watchful and full of recesses into which he could not see. He did not fear the silence; rather he feared that it might suddenly be broken, perhaps by a loud and mirthless laugh. He moved backwards more recklessly, and when he had wriggled through the hole he fairly scampered through the nettles; his legs were stung, but he did not stop running until he had reached the gate. He began to scramble madly over it, but stopped and pretended to lean nonchalantly against it because some people were passing up the lane outside.

He was cross that they had seen him; he did not want to be seen by anybody, and quickly retreated into the long grass by the gatepost. Nevertheless he had had enough of the field, and though his heartbeats were now inaudible again, his mouth felt rather dry. He lurked in the long grass until a cyclist and a pedestrian had passed, both completely unaware of his existence, which gave him some satisfaction. Then he swung over the gate and went up the lane, keeping to the grass verge and trying to look inconspicuous but tough, a secret agent not yet sure of the plot.

He came into the garden by the back way, past the vegetable patch and its lines of rusty carrots. He pulled one up and ate it on the way up to the house. His father was still at work, of course, for it was only about half past three, and his mother had gone out somewhere. 'Oh, you wouldn't want to come, it's only a lot of old women,' she had said; nevertheless, she had dressed very carefully and taken great pains with her hat before she strode off.

Going into the empty house he got himself a glass of water: he put his thumb over the tap so that the water jetted into the glass and frothed, and then gulped it down. Gripping the glass, he screwed up his eyes, nodded, and said aloud to the empty kitchen: 'Now, the theory of this case, as I see it –'

He wasn't yet sure what he was doing. He took out the bottle of vinegar and poured a little into his glass and then jetted water into it: it rose into a pale brown liquid with a satisfactory head of foam on it. Beer, he called it. He sipped his beer and put on a thoughtful expression.

'I'm glad young Beedman's taking this case; he's the most brilliant –' he said aloud again. 'Oh, yes, he's good, he's good.'

He didn't know what to do with himself.

He made himself another glass of beer but it wasn't as exciting as the first one and he poured most of it away, grimacing, and washed the glass.

Now he wanted to go up to the bathroom, but became suddenly more aware of the silence of the house. If there really were people lurking up there, wouldn't they be keeping as quiet as this, just as quiet as this? For some time he leaned against the wall at the bottom of the staircase looking alertly upwards. He could almost imagine he heard the breathing they were trying so hard to suppress. But, at last, he bent the two end fingers of his right hand and extended the first two fingers so that his hand looked like a gun; then he went up the stairs with his gun at the ready and his eyes darting from side to side and got into the bathroom like that.

He had been sitting there for some time, whispering a story to himself about the promising young Royston Beedman, when there was a sudden crash from downstairs and his heart leapt into his throat. He sat there petrified for a long time, but there were no other sounds. Presently he tiptoed out of the bathroom and stood by the top of the stairs, listening. All was quiet. He went back to the bathroom, pulled the chain, and went clattering downstairs, whistling loudly, and stopped as soon as he got to the bottom. There was nobody about. Then he saw that the tumbler he had washed had slid off the edge of a fork on the draining board, in the way things sometimes do when they are drying. That accounted for the crash. He went restlessly round the kitchen and looked out of the back door and wandered into the lounge and fiddled with the *Radio Times*, and then he went straight upstairs and into his parents' bedroom.

It was cooler and darker in there and there was a faint but exciting perfume in the air. He crept over to the wardrobe where his mother's clothes were hung and opened the door a little, and then leafed through her dresses almost as though he

16

were leafing through the pages of a huge book. There was the short black frock she wore sometimes to cocktail parties, and the crêpe frock with flowers on, whose fabric seemed to crawl over the skin of his hand, and the long evening petticoat which rustled when he ran his hand down it; and there was her fur coat. He took a double handful of the fur and rubbed it gently against his cheek and then buried his face in the warm stuff to smell the familiar scent – her face-powder he thought it was.

He went over to the window and peeped out, and then saw that she had spilt some of her powder on the dressing-table. He dabbled the tips of his fingers in it and smelt them pleasurably and then transferred some powder to his cheek and looked in the mirror, but it did not show. He dabbed a little more on his cheeks, but it still did not show. Then he saw her lipstick, the bright scarlet one she sometimes put on in the mornings. He seated himself before the mirror and carefully smeared on a little and then pressed his lips together as he had seen his mother do. When he examined himself in the mirror he was disappointed – the lipstick hardly showed. He put another layer on, thickly, and exaggerated the cupid's bow. Then he leant towards the mirror, drooping his eyelids, and kissed his reflection. 'Royston, darling –' he murmured.

He sat back and looked at himself crossly; he still looked a rather grubby and ridiculous small boy. But – perhaps one of her blouses . . .

In the top drawer he found one of her favourite ones, made of heavy dull silk. He slipped it on and gave his reflection a veiled, sidelong stare. 'You see, Royston,' he murmured, 'I have loved you as long as I can remember.'

He was poking into the jewel-box to find some ear-rings when he was suddenly aware of a rumbling scrunch in the drive.

Merciful God, it was his father!

He snatched up his shirt and rushed into the bathroom and locked the door behind him and tore off the blouse. There was a horrible ripping sound as it came over his shoulders. He filled the basin with water and started scrubbing at the lipstick as he heard his father come into the house.

'Royston!'

The boy made no reply. Oh hell, his father was coming up-stairs. Oh hell oh hell oh hell the lipstick was all over the flannel but there was a lot on his face he couldn't get off. His father rattled the door. 'What the – Royston, are you in there?'

'Yes, Dad.'

'Come out, I'm in a hurry!'

Come off you bastard stuff come off come off you bastard stuff.

'Blast you, Royston, come out, will you: I'm in a hurry.'

'Coming, Dad.'

He stuffed the blouse into one trouser-pocket and the flannel into the other and muffled his face in his handkerchief and then pulled the chain and opened the door and whimpered: 'Sorry, Dad, I –'

But fortunately, his father pushed impatiently past him with-out a glance. Royston darted downstairs to the kitchen sink. Most of the lipstick had come off, but to him his lips still looked suspiciously red. He snatched up some scouring powder and worked with that. Upstairs his father began to walk rapidly from bathroom to bedroom and back. 'Where's your mother?' he called.

'Round at Mrs Maxted's.'

'Oh God, no!'

Upstairs the electric razor started up. Royston put on some more scourer, rinsed it off and examined himself carefully. His lips felt raw and puffy but he couldn't see any traces of lipstick. Now he had to get rid of the blouse that bulged in his pocket; he glanced hastily about and then stuffed it into the dirty-clothes basket and heaped some other clothes on top. The flannel in the other pocket didn't bulge; he thought he could burn it presently.

His father came downstairs in his shirt-sleeves. 'I shall have to ring your mother. What's the number?'

'Francombe two-seven-two.'

'Put a kettle on, will you, I'm in a hurry. We've got to go out. What have you been doing to your face?'

'Well, you see, Dad, I ate some blackberries and –'

'Blackberries?' Mr Beedman stared suspiciously: he didn't think blackberries were in season, but he wasn't quite sure.

However, he strode on to the telephone, and while putting the kettle on Royston heard his father brusquely request his wife to return home – something about an American at London Airport.

Mr Beedman was still upstairs changing when his wife came back. Royston started to lay the table for tea, rather clumsily: he moved stiffly and suddenly felt tired.

He could hear his mother in the bathroom, saying: 'Is this a dressing-up thing?'

'No. We'll take him to the Grape Vine, you know the sort of style. And don't be too long.' Mr Beedman came thundering downstairs. Royston went on putting out plates and keeping an anxious ear cocked; and suddenly stiffened when he heard a drawer jerked open, and heard his mother say: 'Now that's very mysterious. Royston! Have you been at my things?'

'No, Mum,' said Royston instantly.

'Now what the hell's the hold-up?' Mr Beedman demanded.

'I can't find my blouse, the old-gold one; I could have sworn – well, I'll look downstairs, but –'

Royston stood in the kitchen, growing icy cold. His mother came down – she was wearing her tight black skirt but above this had on only a low-cut petticoat. She went straight to the clothes-basket, and in a moment had pulled out the crumpled blouse and held it up. 'But I'm sure I would never have – Oh! Look at this tear, it's ruined! Royston! You little beast! What have you –'

She gave him a furious slap across the face and made his eyes fill with tears.

'Well, you've all been so rotten –' began Royston wildly; and then his father swung his flat hand against the side of the boy's head, sending him reeling into the cooker to cut his forehead open. Royston crouched there for a moment with his mouth open, his face deeply flushed and his eyes glaring at them; then he rushed from the kitchen to his bedroom and flung himself down on his bed, and not until then did the deep sobs begin to force themselves out.

It was through mists of misery and anger that he heard his parents' preparations for departure. One of them, his mother he thought, came to the door of his room and looked in; but he lay obstinately rigid with his head buried in his arms and she went away without a word and soon he heard the car drive off.

A long time afterwards he rolled on to his back and scowled at the ceiling. The cut on his forehead had stopped bleeding but his head felt as though invisible fingers had been stuffed in his ears; he felt very tired and limp, but anger was beginning to pump new energy into him. His mouth set in a grim line and his eyes narrowed, but he was no longer playing at Avengers. Now he *really* wanted revenge. His parents were monsters.

His first plan, to slash his father's clothes to pieces, was followed by a plan to destroy all their belongings and to set fire to the house. But then he thought that for so great a crime, which would be so easily laid at his door, the punishment would, on the evident scale of punishments, be something so frightful that he dared not contemplate it. He began to think of committing the crime and then fleeing beyond the reach of justice; but somehow he knew that in that case he would still be the loser in the end: he would sooner or later be hauled back. Gradually the idea of flight only, without fire-raising, emerged as a satisfactory form of revenge: *how* they would worry, *how* they would wring their hands and tearfully blame themselves for everything. And he would commit no crime; he would merely state, when he was arrested, that he had been driven to this, and then *they* would get into trouble. Yes!

He limped down to the kitchen and ate. He ate savagely, hacking off great slabs of bread, pressing hunks of cheese into his bulging mouth, walking round the kitchen muttering jeeringly to unnamed enemies.

It was dark by the time he finished eating. It seemed terribly late to him and traffic on the main road was becoming intermittent. He opened the back door quietly, shivered, and went back for a pullover. Otherwise he took nothing with him and had no plan. It was a little before ten.

He went cautiously down the garden feeling that hundreds of eyes might be spying out, and his emergence into the lane was a move that took many anxious minutes. But there was no one about, and he slipped more confidently down the lane to the signpost. To the right was the way to Skewley, a walk he knew well; but if he went straight on for four miles he would come to Tipfold, a village just beyond the threshold of his knowledge and therefore tinged with romance. Thither he would go.

By this time he was feeling clear-headed, refreshed, and almost happy. He strode along humming and the night wind ruffled his hair and he even whistled a bit. He had a fright once when a silent owl swooped over his head, and once he had to cower in the ditch while a late cyclist laboured by; but he enjoyed the steady march onward through the mysterious dark and began to believe that fate could not possibly harm him, and any minute now he would be in Tipfold.

But the minutes merged into each other and successive minutes seemed longer and longer and the road still went on; his feet began to ache and when he stopped for a rest he felt cold and shivered. He got a spurt of encouragement from the thought that by now his parents would be frantically running and crying for him; but then a car came slowly along behind him, its headlights sweeping the verges, and he had to cower down again into the ditch, and this time he half hoped he would be found and coddled and taken to a warm place. However, the car passed on and there was nothing for it but to make himself march forward. It was about two o'clock in the morning, he thought: actually it was half past eleven.

He had begun to yawn and weave about and mutter to himself when suddenly out of the darkness loomed the white of the village sign: TIPFOLD. He looked at it unbelievingly and then patted it gratefully and said aloud: 'So there! You see?'

And in that moment he was caught and held in the beam of a police lantern.

3

POLICE Constable Walter Kirby was a young, smart officer with a deep compassion for other people which would probably deny him promotion. He had come out for a last spin on his motor-bike and done the rounds of the pubs at closing time and then driven to this spot for no particular reason except that it was high up and he liked to cast an approving glance over his parish before he turned in. He looked at the white-faced figure in the beam of his torch and said gently: 'Hallo, young feller. And what might you be doing?'

Royston gazed back at him in silence.

'You ought not to be wandering about this time o' night, you know. D'you know what the time is? It's just gone half past eleven.'

Royston's eyes widened momentarily: he had thought it was nearly dawn; but still he said nothing.

'You're not a Tipfold boy, I know; where do you come from, lad?'

Royston suddenly began to feel as though a mailed fist was closing on him; he wanted to bolt, but his legs were trembling violently, and also he was paralysed by the bright light and could not tear himself away. He could not see anything of the face behind the light, but he knew that this was a policeman and the voice sounded kind. Suddenly, however, the voice hardened and became curt – Mr Kirby was trying another tack:

'Don't you try any of your funny stuff on me, my lad! I am a police officer and I am requesting your name and address: speak up!'

Royston was very frightened; he opened his lips but shut them again; his mouth felt dry. The torch moved slightly and came nearer and the voice, which was kind again, said: 'Have you hurt yourself, lad?'

Involuntarily Royston shook his head once, and then resumed his immobile staring, while a large tear crept out of one eye and down his nose. Mr Kirby said, this time in a very gentle voice: 'You look just about done up, son. I think you'd better just come along o' me, eh? Soon have you right.'

Royston made an escaping movement, not really even half a step away, and then stopped and began to blub quietly. The policeman switched his lamp off and patted the boy's shoulder tenderly: Royston couldn't see a thing in a darkness full of swimming lights, but he was aware that the man beside him was tall and smelt faintly of rubber.

'That's a good lad,' said Mr Kirby. 'Soon have you right now. I'll just shove my old bike in under the hedge and then we'll stroll down to my house and see what we can do for you.'

There was a ticking and whirring noise in the darkness as the bike was put away, and then Royston felt the policeman's hand slip under his arm and they set off downhill together.

'You know anything about motor-bikes, son?'

'Not much,' said Royston. They were the first words he had spoken.

'Ah. You didn't see my old bike, I s'pose, but she's a nice little old goer. Velocette 350.'

Royston mumbled something. He was weaving about a bit again, his eyes still not accustomed to the darkness, and every now and then he stumbled against the policeman who strode comfortably, and now rather reassuringly, beside him. He had stopped thinking and was aware only of the support under his arm, the unpredictable gradient of the road beneath his feet and the fading lights in front of his eyes.

They came to a pavement and passed a number of houses and then the policeman guided him up a garden path to a smart new cottage with light streaming from the kitchen window. Mrs Kirby was still up and dressed but had put her hair in curlers and had got the milk on for the cocoa.

' 'Lo, Glad,' said Mr Kirby, wiping his boots carefully on the mat.

' 'Lo,' she said. 'What, we got a visitor, then?'

'Ah. Put another cup on, love.'

Mrs Kirby placidly made two beakersful with the milk she had and then put some more on to heat. She and her husband exchanged a quick glance in which he passed the initiative to her, and she put Royston into a chair by the kitchen table and pushed a beaker over to him. 'Now you sup that up, my lamb, and you'll feel a bit warmer,' she said. 'My, that's a bit of a bump you got there, isn't it; let me have a look at it.'

She pushed back his hair gently and examined the mark on his forehead. 'Ah, 'tis rather a bruise, and it's got a bit of a cut in it, too. I reckon a little bit of iodine on there'll be just the job.'

She went and fetched the bottle and said: 'Don't s'pose you like iodine much, eh? Stings a bit, don't it?'

'A bit,' said Royston, and suddenly smiled at her.

'Ah, it do sting a bit, but only for a minute and it'll fetch down that bruise. There! The heavyweight champion after the fight.'

Royston grinned and blushed faintly and sipped his cocoa. 'I expect 'twas a bit cold out, warn't it?' she said. 'Have you come far?'

'Francombe,' he said, rather proudly.

'Francombe? My word! that must be a good walk, all of five miles, nearly six; you come from the Old Town?'

'No. New.'

He was feeling warmer and more wideawake and as though the adventure were now over and it was fun to tell Mum about it. He was only distantly aware of the policeman, who was quietly pottering about, mixing his own drink, looking at the boiler; but listening.

'Would you like a biscuit with your drink, er – er – there now, I didn't catch your name?'

'Beedman – Royston Beedman,' said Royston, without thinking.

'Oh, ah. Well, have a biscuit, Royston, and I'll have one, too.'

So they settled down amicably munching and presently the policeman came and sat down at the table too, and asked quietly: 'What you run away for, son?'

Royston was carrying a biscuit to his mouth at the time. His hand stopped, then went on more slowly and he choked on the biscuit and took another sip of drink and said: 'Didn't run away. Just went for a walk and then sort of – well, went too far.'

'Ah, that's true. How did you bump your head?'

'I bumped it on something. In the dark.'

'M'm? No one hit you?'

'No!'

'Ah, well. Mum and Dad know where you are, then?'

'No,' whispered Royston.

'They'll be worried about you, then, won't they?'

'No. I mean yes. I dunno.'

'H'm. Hadn't been no row at all, no trouble at home like?'

'No! 'Course not. Just went for a walk, that's all.'

The policeman propped his head on his hand and gazed a long time at the little white face opposite. Royston's eyes dropped before this scrutiny and he took some more sips of his drink. Mr Kirby sighed deeply and said: 'Ah, well. We better let your Dad know you've been found. What's his address, son?'

Reluctantly the boy answered: 'Twelvetrees, Grange Road, Francombe.'

'Is he on the phone?'

'Francombe two-seven-oh.'

The policeman wrote this down in his notebook. 'What's your full name?' he asked.

'Royston Carter Beedman.'

'And your age?'

'Twelve.'

The policeman wrote this down also, and then lumbered over to the door of his office, unlocked it, and went in to use the phone. Royston sat very quietly; so did Mrs Kirby, who was now knitting in a ruminative way. Royston felt sleepy and rather small and could think of nothing but the sensation of stretching his legs out in a freshly-made bed. Through the door he could hear the muffled tones of Mr Kirby asking for the Francombe number, then there was a long pause and then the receiver was replaced. No reply, evidently. Mr Kirby asked for another Francombe number.

'Ah – Tipfold police here,' he said. 'Oh, hallo, George ... can't grumble, and you? ... Ah. George, I've picked up a young lad here, found wandering, name of Beedman, Royston Beedman – no, Beedman, B double E – Twelvetrees, Grange Road, has he been reported? ... Oh. Odd. I rang the house, but no reply. What's the set-up there, George, d'you know? ... Oh, you don't? No. ... That's very good of you, George; you're sure it's not out of his way? Good. I'll hang on here, then, and you chase the father over. Thanks very much, George – cheeroh, then.'

Mr Kirby came back to the kitchen. 'Well, you'd better get to bed, Glad,' he said. 'No point in waiting up. I'll put Tiger Tim here on the couch till his Dad comes.'

'All right. Wrap him in this rug, Walter – no, here, let me do it. You men!'

So Royston was wrapped up and draped along the settee, where he fell instantly asleep, and Mrs Kirby went up to bed, where she fell into a light spasmodic doze, and Mr Kirby settled down at the kitchen table and thoughtfully rolled a cigarette; and the light airs that spring up after midnight blew about the silent village.

It was well past one o'clock in the morning when a car came accelerating noisily down the street and past the police cottage, only to brake sharply and then back in. Mr Kirby went to his front door under the lamp and watched the pudgy figure in the flapping overcoat bustle out with his wife behind him. Mr Beedman was frightened but aggressive; during the evening he had spent too much on drink for the American without getting the concession he wanted.

'Now what the devil's all this, officer?' he began.

'Mr Beedman, is it?' said the policeman imperturbably. 'If you'd just step into the office for a moment, sir?'

'Oh, God, no bloody red tape now! Let's have the kid and get home. It's late and I've got work to do.'

'So have I, sir, indeed.' Walter ushered them into the office and took his time over settling at the deal table with the log-book on it. Mr Beedman did not sit down; his wife did, with a certain weary hauteur.

'What's your version of tonight's affair, sir?'

'Version? I've got no version, I don't know what's happened yet.'

'You've been out for the evening?'

'Of course. What of it?'

'And the boy was alone in the house?'

'He'd gone to bed and was asleep before we left.'

'But he was alone in the house?'

'So what? There's no law against it.'

'There is, sir; but we'll say no more about that for the moment. Has the boy ever wandered off like this before?'

'Certainly not, of course not, never a moment's anxiety.'

Walter had picked up a pencil and was gently tapping it on his fingernails, staring down thoughtfully. Then he said: 'How did he come by that lump on his head, sir?'

There was an abrupt and noticeable silence; both the Beedmans had stopped breathing. Walter gazed into Mr Beedman's eyes, which were like brown marbles. Mr Beedman licked his lips rapidly once and said: 'Now what cock-and-bull story has he been telling you?'

'The boy's not said very much about it, sir.'

'He stooped suddenly,' said Mr Beedman. 'He stooped to pick up something, a – er – a piece of a large jigsaw he has, a picture of Glamis Castle as a matter of fact. And so, of course, as he went down he caught his forehead on the edge of the table, rather a nasty crack, quite upset the wife as a matter of fact; but no tears, no fuss at all, very good really.'

Tap, tap, tap went the pencil; but Walter was thinking, not of Mr Beedman's story, but of how much of a fuss Mr Beedman could make at the Divisional Office if his account was now challenged. Well, it wouldn't be of much help in any case, either to Royston or to Walter himself; he put the pencil down and rose to his feet. It was, after all, two o'clock in the morning.

'Well, thank you very much for being so patient, sir,' said Walter. 'You'll appreciate that I have to make the prescribed inquiries in these matters.'

'No, I'm afraid I fail to see why you have to.'

'Just so, sir,' said Walter meaninglessly. 'Now if you'd wait one moment, sir, I'll fetch the lad in.'

27

Royston presently appeared in a stunned and blinking condition and Walter noticed that the boy did not glance at his father but gave a quick imploring look at his mother, whose expression was one of icy fury. Walter put his hand gently on the boy's shoulder. 'Now, Royston,' he said, 'trot along home with your Mum and Dad and don't let me ever catch you wandering round again at night. O.K.?'

The boy bobbed his head and slunk off into the night, followed by his parents, without another word spoken. The policeman stood in his porch and watched them climb into the car, which was turned round viciously and taken roaring off up the street. Walter shook his head sadly after them; looked round the sky, wound his watch, sighed, and went to bed.

Royston dozed fitfully on the way back, resting his cheek against the cool glass of the window and jerking awake when they slammed round a sharp corner. Awake and dozing he was continuously aware of the whiteness of the head-lamps battering against the hedgerows.

During his first short waking period he heard his father's voice muttering something unintelligible in the terrifying snarl that meant loss of self-control, and his mother replying wearily: 'It won't do any good, Gilbert, let's get to bed.'

As they cornered savagely into Grange Road, Royston heard his father say: 'I told you it'd turn out like this, didn't I? I told you at the time. I told you not to do it.' Do what? thought Royston, blearily.

The car rumbled to a stop at last and Mr Beedman jerked the door open and in silence pointed at the house. Royston ran on the tips of his toes through the kitchen and up the stairs to his bedroom and whipped off his clothes in a jumble, wrenching madly at his shoe-laces, and dived into bed with the blankets pulled over his head, lying there stiff and immobile, waiting to see if he was pursued, the blood throbbing in his ears. Presently the throbbing changed to a tired and distant singing; and he slept.

He slept long after his father had rushed, blue-jowled, off to work. He slept long after his mother, who had been crouching miserably in a corner of the bed, got up and took a tablet and fell into a frowning slumber. He slept long after Police Constable Kirby walked, freshly-shaven, into his office and began to type. While Royston slept, Mr Kirby, typing quite quickly and well, wrote:

PERKHAMPTON CONSTABULARY

Division:	Francombe
Date:	4 August 1954
Officer:	P.C.479 Kirby W.

Superintendent,

1. At 11.33 p.m. on Tuesday 3 August, while patrolling in the village of Tipfold, P.C. Kirby observed and stopped a boy who appeared to be wandering in a distressed condition.

2. On being taken to the Police House, this boy gave his name as ROYSTON CARTER BEEDMAN, aged 12, of Twelvetrees, Grange Road, Francombe; and further stated that he had been for a walk, but had wandered too far.

3. As a result of inquiries made by telephone and in person by P.Act.S. Kerridge, it was established that there was nobody at the boy's home address at 11.50 p.m., 12.15 a.m., and 12.45 a.m. The boy's father, GILBERT BEEDMAN, was eventually contacted at 1.25 a.m. when he returned to his home from London, and after a short interview was persuaded by A/Sgt. Kerridge to fetch his son from Tipfold.

4. Father and son were interviewed by P.C. Kirby, and both maintained that the boy, ROYSTON, had simply wandered away from home and become tired. MR BEEDMAN then resumed charge of his son at 2.05 a.m. on 4 August.

(Signed) W. M. Kirby
P.C.479, Francombe Division

'Is that all you're going to put, love?' Mrs Kirby had been sweeping the office and paused to look over his shoulder.

Walter shrugged. 'All I can put, isn't it? That's the only facts there are, poor little devil. I don't know what the Super will say – prob'ly tell me I been wasting paper and dock it out of me pay.'

But the Superintendent did no such thing. He frowned at the report for half a minute; and then he brusquely ordered a copy to be sent to the County Children's Officer.

4

On the London side of Francombe, the main road runs across a dull, flat plain. On one side of the road lie monotonous fields of cabbage and beet; on the other are the gravel pits. These form a wasteland of raw umber-coloured diggings, grass-covered spoil heaps and trenches, queer rattling contrivances in corrugated-iron towers and clumps of dusty thorn trees.

Royston had occasionally been there before, but the torrent of traffic roaring down the main road was so perilous that he preferred usually to wander in the opposite direction. But today, the first time he'd been out since his Tipfold adventure, he had decided that it might be safer to go in an unusual direction. He waited for a long time on the grass verge opposite the workings, fearing that at any moment he would be arrested from behind, impatiently watching the incessant stream of cars making for the coast; and when at last there came a gap, there would be a maddening van coming in the opposite direction to prevent his crossing. But at last he had a space and he scuttled across like a little khaki rabbit and through the gap in the hedge and dropped thankfully into a shallow trench littered with paper bags and smelling of urine. He crouched there for a bit and began to recover his self-respect.

On the Wednesday, after his flight to Tipfold, he had slept until noon, and was awakened by the sound of coffee cups being rattled about in the kitchen. He lay for some time trying to deduce what might happen next; he didn't feel himself to be hungry, but his mind seemed to be slightly detached from his body, like a soap-bubble clinging to the side of a bubble-pipe. Presently he had to get up, and when he clattered out of the bathroom the sounds in the kitchen stopped abruptly. There followed a prolonged silence; Royston stood by his bedroom door with his ears straining, and evidently his mother was standing equally motionless in the kitchen. Royston could visualize her upturned, vindictive face. She was the one who moved first, racing upstairs with her housecoat rustling.

'What are you doing?'

'Nothing, Mum. Dressing.'

'Well, get dressed then.'

She went downstairs again, and when he was dressed Royston went down rather humbly after her. She sat sipping coffee and nibbling dry toast and did not look at him. He waited uncertainly and then went to the coffee pot on the stove.

'What are you doing?' she barked.

Royston jumped. 'Please could I have some coffee, Mum?'

'No! You'll have what you're given! Sit down in the corner.'

Royston sat down with his face slowly flushing crimson. After a minute and a half she said: 'D'you know what you are? Do you? You're an undisciplined, ungrateful, irresponsible little – little – well, that's what you are. And the sooner you realize that, and the sooner you do something about it, the better it'll be for you. D'you understand? Do you? Answer me. Answer me!'

'Yes, Mum,' said Royston.

'And don't you dare grin at me!'

Involuntarily Royston had let an embarrassed half-smile creep on to his face. He wiped it off again. She looked ghastly white and her eyes were jerking, and it was with a horrified pleasure that Royston recognized that he was to some extent satisfied with her distress.

They sat in silence for another five minutes and then Royston made a slight movement and she snapped: 'Where are you going?'

Royston started to mumble 'Out in the garden', but before he had begun, she said:

'Well, you can't! Sit still. You'll only do what you're told in future, understand?'

So Royston sat there mutinously fidgeting his feet about and after five minutes she said: 'Oh, for God's sake stop it, haven't you any damned consideration? Go and read a book or something.'

He spent the rest of that day in the lounge, ostensibly reading, occasionally lying on his back muttering his own stories to himself. He turned the radio on once, but she immediately swept in and turned it off with a violent jerk, fixing him with a glare. He found a dark corner of the room and tore a bit of wallpaper off; then he started to work on the plaster underneath, which was dry and came off in little crumbs. He also worked a hole in the base of the settee and extracted a fair amount of the stuffing, throwing it out of the french window under the fuchsia bush. He worked on these two projects when he could, while his mother mooned about in her housecoat, nibbling chocolates. He kept his resentment on half-throttle because he knew he still had to face his father. But Mr Beedman drove homeward in such a filthy temper that he felt thoroughly fed-up, so he stopped at the roadhouse on the corner for a few drinks and then dined there; and when he did come back, Royston was in bed and the lack-lustre meal Mrs Beedman had prepared was spoilt and there was a furious whining row between them. Royston lay in the darkness and hugged himself.

The next day, Thursday, neither of his parents spoke to him at all, not one word. He worked for a while on the plaster in the lounge but this presently bored him so he got his jigsaw and pretended that the pieces were soldiers, which he drilled and campaigned with quite happily, turning them over if they were shot. In the afternoon Mrs Maxted and Mrs Lyle and Sally Driver came for bridge and Royston was locked in his bedroom. He tried to escape down the drainpipe, but it was a long stretch from the window and the height made him giddy. He tried making a rope of knotted sheets, and went so far as to dangle one out of the window, but every knot he tried to tie came slithering undone; so in the end he unpicked some of the plaster from the wall under his bed and had his jigsaw pieces as miners carrying plaster on their backs. His evening meal was brought to him on a tray.

The next morning his mother was in a more amicable mood and they talked a bit and went out in the garden together. Royston felt rather sorry for the distress he had caused her and wanted to show this in some way; and after a long hesitation he impulsively grabbed hold of her hand and tried to squeeze it. But she froze so, and threw off his hand with such a shudder of distaste, that he felt completely mortified and withdrew into a mood of sullen boorishness, and his snarls raised a prickle of temper in her again. She was in a quandary : she was due at Mrs Lyle's that afternoon and had intended to take Royston with her, but she felt she could not take this ill-mannered brat, yet she could not leave him to wander off from an unguarded house.

In the end she locked up all his clothes and went off, leaving him in the house naked.

When the door slammed behind her, Royston sat on the edge of his bed with tears running down his flushed cheeks. Up to that moment he had not believed his parents could do such a thing to him. He darted to the landing window and watched her go out of the gate without a backward glance, and then he rushed back to his room, flung himself down on the bed, stuffed a corner of the counterpane into his mouth and sobbed and sobbed and presently fell asleep.

When he awoke the rays of sunshine were slanting horizontally and he felt cold. There were no sounds from downstairs. He put his pyjamas on and got into bed properly, watching the patches of sunlight on the wall and planning his revenge, which he did by speaking aloud to some imaginary but attentive listener, a newspaper reporter perhaps.

'So you see, I decided at an early date – it was in August of that year, as a matter of fact – that what I had to do was –'

He paused. What had he got to do? Get out of it; that was the urgent thing, get out of it. He gazed under drowsy eyelids at the patches on the wall. Either he could just run away, or he could do something awful that would make them put him out. Yes, that sounded better, somehow, he'd know where he stood; but what could he do?

When his mother came up he feigned sleep; he heard her say, 'Thank God for that anyway,' as she closed the door softly behind her. He sneered at the door and raised two fingers. Soon after this he fell genuinely asleep, with nothing decided except that somehow he ought to rouse his father to a pitch of high fury – his father was probably the one most likely to turn him out.

But, alas, next morning Mr Beedman was in towering high spirits; had a hot bath before breakfast, always a good sign, and came down flushed and jolly. He had secured a very promising import agency, the big coup of the year so far.

'Know what I did yesterday?' he said to his wife, kissing a hollow beside her neck with a squelching sound. 'Got you a mink wrap. They're making it up for me now.'

He chose many of his wife's clothes himself.

'And as for young Samson here, well, if he's a good lad, it's a bicycle for him.'

'For God's sake, Gilbert, after all that's happened –' Mrs Beedman showed no pleasure over the wrap and only anger over this.

'Oh, damn everything that's happened, let bygones be bygones, that's what I say. Boys will be boys; boy myself once. This is a big thing, Tina, you don't seem to realize.'

And Mr Beedman fetched some more coffee, singing: 'Ho, the flies crawl up the window, dah dah di-dah dah dah.' Royston looked at him with stony eyes; he felt quite nauseated.

Mr Beedman's good temper continued. He sent Royston out for some cigarettes and didn't check the change; and before lunch he went up to the Golf Club for some drinks and came back beaming. In the afternoon he proposed to take his wife to a cocktail party in St John's Wood, so he gave Royston five bob and sent him off to the pictures; Royston did not thank him but added the coins to the florin he'd kept out of the cigarette-money and went off as fast as he could to the gravel-pits before his mother, in her disapproval, could stop him.

So now he sat in the trench and mused. He could not have said, if asked, that he had reached a turning point in his life; but in fact, up to this time he had philosophically endured rough times at home, knowing that smooth times often followed, and when they did he made the best use he could of them, knowing that they wouldn't last long. Probably he had gradually been growing less and less tolerant of bribes and punishments, but anyway, whether slowly or abruptly, here he

34

was, still resolved, despite his father's generous offer, to hold out against the whole boiling of them. He wasn't going to give in just for a bike – as in the past he had given in for a watch and a football and a train set and, far back, for a pedal car.

After about half an hour Royston felt cramped and restive, so he went up to the Transport Café and bought some crisps and then trailed off towards the pits munching and hoping to find an old tyre to fool about with. He was passing some rusty oil-drums by a thorn tree when a hand suddenly gripped his ankle and brought him down with a cry.

'That bloody 'ad yer, didn't it?'

Royston stared back at the dark-haired boy with the heart-shaped face who had made a den among the oil-drums. 'You've made me spill my crisps,' he said bitterly.

'You got some crisps, 'ave yer? Cor, less 'ave a look.'

They poked about in the dirty grasses retrieving the crisps; what the boy found, he ate. He seemed to feel that he was breaking etiquette, and should offer something in return, for when the crisps were all eaten he said: 'Wanna look at my place?'

Royston nodded and followed him around the oil-drums. It was quite ingenious: the boy had scraped out a hole in the ground, put a corrugated iron roof on it and covered that with sand, and then artistically littered oil-drums about to shield the entrance of the artificial cave.

He was gratified by Royston's admiring glance.

''Ave a fag,' he said.

'Thanks,' said Royston.

It was rather noisome in the cave; better to recline in the entrance with one's legs inside and puff sophisticatedly into the air. Royston felt slightly dizzy and had dribbled into his cigarette, for he rarely smoked.

'Smoke much?' asked the boy.

'No,' said Royston.

'Not like me, then. I'm an 'eavy smoker; ten a day, twenty a day, like that. I bet I smoke more'n any other boy at our school. I can't give it up, yer see; it's an 'abit.'

Royston was not sure of the correct reply and remained silent.

'You don't go to Boulton Road, do yer?'

'No,' said Royston. 'I go to boarding school.'

'Do yer? To the special school?'

'Well, it's fairly special, I suppose.'

'No, no, I mean the daft school, that sort of special.'

'Oh, no!'

The boy seemed impressed. 'Wot's yer name?'

'Beedman. What's yours?'

'Tod. You got any money?'

'A bit,' said Royston cautiously.

'Give us it; I'll go and get a mineral.'

Royston gave him the florin and Tod went to the café and brought back a large bottle of raspberryade and a packet of five Woodbines. They drank and belched loudly and lit up again, though Royston didn't particularly want another smoke.

'You can be my mate if you like,' said Tod. 'Where d'yer live?'

'In the New Town.'

'I live in Fish Lane. I'm boarded out.'

'Whatever's that?'

'Boarded out: you know, don't yer? I got a foster-mother.'

Royston gazed admiringly at this romantic figure. 'Haven't you got any parents?' he asked.

'Somewhere,' shrugged Tod. 'Least, I've got a mum. She wasn't married.'

'Coo! How did you find out?'

''Ad a dekko at me birth sustificate, o' course,' said Tod scornfully. 'That's wot I did.'

There was a pause while Royston absorbed this staggering news, and nonchalantly stubbed out his half-smoked fag. 'What's it like, having a foster-mother?' he asked.

'Terrible!' cried Tod. 'Cor, don't you ever be! Do this, do that, fetch the coal in, scrub the floors. I get flogged every night!'

'Do you?'

'Yer! Wiv a whip. And then she rubs salt in.'

'Coo!'

'It's ghastly.'

'But can't you tell somebody about it?'

'Oh, I will; when my time comes, I shall tell everybody. Yer! I'll shop the ole bag, I'm only biding me time.' Tod nodded darkly.

'Couldn't you run away?'

'Yers. I might do that too, when my time comes.'

'Where would you run away to, Tod?'

'Up London. That's the place, they'd never find you there.'

'But where could you hide?'

'Ooh, there's plenty o' places up London, all them little alleys. Trafalgar Square, that's a good place; you know Trafalgar Square? I know Trafalgar Square very well, I'm often up there. Loads o' little alleys round Trafalgar Square, where you could 'ide.'

Royston plucked a bit of grass and thoughtfully chewed the arid stem. 'You'd have to have some money; would you try and get a job?'

'No!' snarled Tod contemptuously. 'Listen: do you believe in pinching?'

This was a trick question: Royston didn't like to answer either yes or no. He gained time by producing an artificial belch and Tod resumed: 'I'm a good pincher, I am, I bet there's nobody in our school comes up to me for pinchin'. Well, there's plenty o' fur coats up London, all the tarts 'ave one; knock off a few fur coats an' flog 'em, then yer quids in. Live in a hotel then, no one'd know.'

'The police would get you!'

'Ah, they're stupid!'

There was a long silence; each boy was following a line of thought. Royston had not accepted Tod's detailed ideas, but the general policy was an attractive one. Tod was obviously a knowledgeable fellow and Royston wondered whether he could confide in him and get him to help – perhaps they could go off together; there was something reassuring in having a companion. Royston had opened his mouth to speak when Tod, glancing sideways, said: 'Good 'ere, ain't it?'

'Yes.'

'Nice and quiet. Tell yer wot we'll do next: you strip off.'

'No!' cried Royston.

'Yer, go on – you strip off and then I tie you up. Reelly tight!'

'No!' Royston felt alarmed, this boy was heavier than he was; he prepared for a fight.

'I love tyin' up. One o' these days I'll get that young welfare lady wot comes to see me an' I'll tie her up. And gag her. And then I'll – I'll –'

Tod's eyes were shining as he struggled to express in words his lurid dream. Royston felt the situation to be tense; he glanced anxiously about and then said: 'Let's take the bottle back and get the money on it.'

Reluctantly Tod abandoned his dream. 'All right,' he said. 'Go 'alves?'

'All right.'

They went back to the café and solemnly shared the tuppence-on-the-bottle and then a constraint fell between them because Royston wanted to break away now but did not wish to offend his new mate. They stood beside the lay-by outside the café scuffling their shoes in the dust, not knowing what to do next, and then fortunately a van pulled up sharply alongside and the driver called: ''Allo, Toddy boy! Wanna lift 'ome?'

'Yeah, sure!' said Tod, delighted. 'See ya!' he called carelessly over his shoulder to Royston, scrambled into the van and drove off home to the decent little woman who looked after him.

Royston recrossed the main road without difficulty now that the traffic had slackened. He wandered towards his home by a devious route, gradually drawing closer, now hurrying and now dawdling. His feelings had become mixed. On the one side, he felt that he had escaped earlier from confinement in a place that he loathed; he had revelled in his freedom, and Tod had put up all sorts of thoughts about paradise over the horizon; escape from this bewildering situation that took so much coping with, the chance of regaining Face. But there was something else, too. Tod had suggested to him an exciting possibility: perhaps there was some mystery about *his* parents! In some obscure way he felt that if he could only find out he would have a powerful weapon to use against them. Sometimes he hurried to find out quickly, sometimes he dawdled to savour every possibility and to put off learning the truth.

At last, however, he realized that if his parents were at a cocktail party they might be home before long and he would have to make his investigation quickly: it was unthinkable that he could discover anything while they were there, even more so that he could just ask them. Birth sustificate, Tod had said; Royston broke into a run and arrived back in the silent house breathless, with his heart thudding.

Birth sustificate. Some kind of document, he supposed. Now where would it be? He went across to the bureau in the lounge and skimmed rapidly through the papers in the pigeon holes. He didn't quite know what he was looking for, but there was nothing here that had any reference to himself at all. He replaced the papers carefully, something telling him that he needed to cover his tracks.

Where else! Oh hurry, where else? Nothing in the bureau drawers, nothing in the sideboard drawer, nothing in the tea-caddy thing where his mother kept the insurance policies. Some things she kept in her handbag, but she had that with her. Oh, hurry! Upstairs! She had forgotten to lock her door against him this time; he went quickly through her jewel boxes, nothing there, nothing in the writing-case by her bedside. Oh, hurry, hurry, surely there could be nothing in the wardrobe.

But on the shelf at the top of the wardrobe, in a corner hidden by her hats, was another box, a deedbox – he now remembered vaguely having seen it, incuriously, once before when he was prying about. He got it down with trembling hands. Birth certificate – Christine Brenda Carter, now who on earth – oh, of course. Now this one, this one –

He read the sprawling writing in columns from left to right: Fifteenth May 1942, England. Royston Carter Beedman. Male. Gilbert Everard Beedman, 17 Abbey Ponds Road, Chipham, Company director, and Christine Brenda Beedman of the same address, housewife.

Royston experienced a sinking feeling, more and more with each entry he spelt out. This was all right; there was no mystery; there were his name and his parents' names just as he had always known they'd be.

Next column: Sixteenth November, 1942. Court of Summary Jurisdiction for the Urban District of Chipham. Now what the devil was this? Royston's glance skittered all over the certificate seeking a clue to this court business, and as he did so, one word sizzled into his brain: ADOPTED.

His breath came out in a long sigh and he slowly spelt out the message at the bottom of the form: 'CERTIFIED to be a true copy of an entry in the Adopted Children Register maintained at the General Register Office.'

Royston folded the certificate slowly and carefully and put it back exactly as he had found it.

5

ROYSTON'S second flight from his home was not a spur-of-the-moment action. He thought it over, or rather he mused over it, lying in the bath telling himself long stories, either in dialogue or as a running commentary delivered by some omniscient observer. Out of each long, muttered story some part of a plan would emerge either as practicable, to be accepted, or ridiculous, to be rejected. But it was slow going and at one time he became so depressed with the difficulties and discomforts of running away that he gave up the plan altogether and decided to wait till he was older.

This was on the Monday. On the Tuesday his 'father' (the inverted commas were now clear in Royston's mind) came home early and discovered the hacked-out hole in the wall of the lounge. Mr Beedman became helpless with anger, his throat clenched, his face suffusing with blood, his little feet pawing the carpet. Royston was frightened, but not so terrified as he might have been a fortnight earlier: his feelings had become peculiarly diluted since he had found out that he was not related to this ridiculous man. So he kept his poker-face for some time, till Mr Beedman suddenly rushed upstairs, panting with fury and crying: 'I'll show you what it's like, then, you little fool; you smash up my things and I'll smash up yours, perhaps that'll teach you what it's like.' He went into Royston's bedroom and got the cricket bat and tried to break it over his knee but couldn't, so he wedged it in the radiator and put his weight on it and so splintered the handle out of the blade and stood with a chunk of wood in each hand and his hair sticking out sideways, glaring at Royston, and saying: 'There! How d'you like it, eh, how do you like it? Perhaps that'll teach you to have a bit of respect for property!' It was hard then to keep the poker-face; but Royston managed it, though his eyes brimmed with tears, for he had been fond of the bat, which Mr Beedman had given him less than a month previously.

He was now quite resolved to take himself away from people with whom he obviously had no connexion whatsoever; and he fell once more to musing over his problems. His main problem was where to run to. He had no aunts, uncles or cousins that he knew of – not that he thought this out; he was simply unaware of these relationships. There was a vague grandfather person somewhere whom Mr Beedman visited but always by himself and very rarely. He knew he had to get away from Francombe, which ruled out the lady in the pet-shop who was always kind to him. Various people floated into his mind at this stage, half-remembered figures from long ago – a lady in a hairdresser's who gave him a sweet while he waited, a jolly bus-conductor at Whipsnade who once winked at him, a lady in an office somewhere who had let him work her typewriter. Royston had no friends. In the dormitory at school he slept next to Gunter and he and Gunter had talked together quite a lot, but except that Gunter lived in Bournemouth he knew very little about him. Royston hadn't been long at his present school anyway; before it he had been at a Primary School in Croydon, where he could only remember being lonely in the crowded playground, and before that he had been to Miss Mee's school for about twelve children; and before that to a half-remembered school that was very noisy and surrounded by railings. But in none of these had he found a friend. Several times he thought wistfully about Tod; Tod was a swashbuckling, competent character, up against the world as he was himself. Nevertheless, there were objections to Tod: he was not an instantly likeable boy and some of his statements had somehow rung a little false – he might well prove to be a broken reed. Reluctantly Royston came to the conclusion that this time he'd got to go it alone.

The dazzling shock of his discovery by the Tipfold policeman had left him with the knowledge that great eyes would everywhere be watching for him, even in the most remote and silent glens. He felt that a small boy alone would attract instant attention; this was the objection to Trafalgar Square, however highly Tod might recommend it, for Royston could not imagine a plausible reason why he should be wandering about alone in that crowded concourse, and he would therefore be conspicuous. Somehow he had to become inconspicuous. He toyed for a while with the idea of a disguise, but it did not stand up to a muttered cross-examination in the bathroom. So he mused on until he hit on what was really a very good idea, which was to make for the seaside. He realized that the seaside was one place where children are always wandering about alone, often carrying suitcases, and if challenged he could always say naturally that he had come down for the day and that his parents were 'somewhere over there' amongst that crowd of people. Besides, there was something both safe and fascinating about the sea itself. So he resolved to run away to the sea, and the only place he knew was East Whixham, so he fixed upon that.

His next problem was to get money for the journey, which was not easy in that house because his 'parents' paid most things by cheque, and it was virtually impossible to get at the money carried round in an impregnable handbag and an almost never seen light-brown wallet. He took to skulking about downstairs in the mornings in a state like that of an anxious sleeper waiting for an alarm-clock to go off; at the first hint that the coast was clear he would dart silently into the kitchen, open the handbag, snatch one coin, and dart out again. It was anxious, perturbing work; in the mornings the 'daily woman' was about, plodding silently round in her slippers, but when she had the vacuum-cleaner going, and Mrs Beedman was upstairs, dressing or in the bathroom, he could pull off a noiseless, darting coup and escape with his heart thudding. Thus he accumulated six-and-six, which he hid amongst the pieces of a jigsaw in a box.

Once his preparations had been made, he could have been triggered off at any time, and this finally happened on the Friday afternoon. Mrs Beedman was due at Sally Driver's for a séance, and remembering what had apparently worked very well before, she again took Royston's clothes away, locked them up in her bedroom and went off without a backward glance. The indignity set Royston moving. He had prepared for this eventuality by hiding a set of clothes under the mattress in the spare bedroom. They were things he reckoned would not be

43

missed: old things of his, the shirt frayed and the trousers decidedly tight. Within ten minutes of his 'mother's' departure he was dressed and had rooted out some old plimsolls from the boot cupboard under the stairs. He fetched the small attaché case he had hidden in the greenhouse and loaded it with some raw bacon, some buns, a jar of jam and a spoon, a half-empty box of chocolates and a slab of jelly. He also put in a silver christening-mug and a musical cigarette box in the shape of a chalet, which he had been told never to touch as it was valuable; and, as a last-minute addition, a scarf from the hall in case he got cold. At a quarter past two he slipped furtively out of the house, so furtively that he must have aroused suspicion had anyone been passing, and trotted determinedly down to the station.

Getting the ticket was a nerve-racking business, for the man seemed appallingly suspicious. Royston asked for a half-single to East Whixham and was about to add a nonchalant remark about 'just slipping down for the day', when the man said: 'Are you fourteen?'

Royston was not expecting this question, and he blushed to the roots of his hair and looked the picture of guilt. 'Yes,' he stammered confusedly. 'No, I mean no, I'm twelve.'

He was poised to bolt for it at that moment, but the man grunted and gave him his ticket and he escaped thankfully on to the platform. He had one-and-ninepence left.

He was too nervous to ask a porter about trains, and could not understand the incomprehensible squawking that came out of the loudspeakers, so he missed the first train, and when it pulled out from the empty platform he felt as exposed as an ant on a plate. He hid himself in a waiting-room and presently recovered his nerve; he boarded the next train correctly and was whisked away to the seaside without further incident.

He emerged confidently from East Whixham Central, marched straight down to the front, set down his case and leant on the railings gazing calmly at the sea. It was a windy, changeable day, more like April than August, with clouds blowing across the sun so that the sea was sometimes a sparkling blue and sometimes a chill grey. He felt very much at home. He had

44

no clear plan of campaign, but he was now experiencing no twinges of guilt or furtiveness and strolled placidly along the front. During one sunny period he bought an orange lolly and wished he had been able to bring his swimming trunks. He went down on the beach to finish his lolly and was presently beguiled into making a battleground in the sand with matchboxes for tanks. This game soon absorbed him and he squatted there, muttering incessantly to himself as he imitated the R/T; it ceased suddenly when he realized that he was hungry, and he looked up to find the beach almost deserted.

He moved up under the sea-wall and thoughtfully ate two buns and half the slab of jelly; he realized that he had now got to start planning again. He had no idea what the time was, but everyone seemed to have gone off for tea or bed or both, and only two distant figures were sauntering by the grey and ebbing sea. He realized that he had become conspicuous again, but huddled there for some time in a blank mood, feeling that movement would draw attention to himself. Later he changed his tactics and marched briskly along the promenade, thinking that he might escape notice if he seemed to be going somewhere. Nobody seemed to notice him, however, let alone challenge him; the prom was filled with short fat men in grey tweed suits, caps and plimsolls, aimlessly escorting amply-built women clutching coats to their throats, for the breeze had stiffened with the falling tide. Some of the lights came on; Royston's pace slowed and he stopped to examine a booth full of small brass lighthouses. Then he bought some candyfloss and looked at some boxing-comics on a stall. He was putting off making any sort of decision.

The need for a decision was finally brought home to him when he saw a policeman in a white coat, directing traffic near the Marina Tower. The crowd on the prom had thinned and the sea was murmuring in the darkness. Royston began to feel depressed and frightened and realized that he must find a den to crawl into; he started to hurry along the front, looking anxiously about and praying for inspiration.

He found it when he came to a long row of beach-huts: after a hasty glance all round, he scrambled over the railing and dropped on to the sand and then scuttled in under the nearest one, which was raised on legs above the dry and shifting sand. There he crouched, peering out with glittering eyes, like a hedgehog in a ditch. It was a peculiar place; the sand was dry but unexpectedly cold and full of orange peel, cigarette packets, baked seaweed and wood.

He passed a dreadful night. He got very cold and the scarf was little help; he covered his legs and stomach with sand, which did seem to help, but couldn't cover his shoulders, and so regularly awoke from a fitful doze with his teeth chattering. The night was full of peculiar noises, as though the whole beach was secretly sliding down; and presently the incoming tide intruded into his crowded dreams and made them even more urgent. He woke with a jump somewhere around six when somebody in gumboots, a boatman of some sort, squelched past his beach-hut. Royston clutched himself in terror until the footsteps faded, and then dozed off again. When he again woke, red-eyed and limp, it was raining.

He rolled on to his stomach and gazed blearily at the sodden beach; it was a sight he had never dreamed could exist. He felt extremely lonely and could not imagine what he thought he was achieving by all this; had Mr Beedman appeared at that moment, Royston would have gone back with him like a lamb. However, the experience of being under cover and watching rain falling outside always gives one a cosy feeling, however bleak the cover may be; presently he began to feel more optimistic and even to experience a strange excitement over his situation, a feeling that this was unique, nobody knew where he was, and no one was sharing all this with him. He ate the raw bacon, tearing it away from the rind with his teeth. It tasted salty and rather queer and was appropriate to his mood. He finished it and then he finished the chocolates and then he resolved to spend part of his last sevenpence on a cup of tea, for he was feeling quite thirsty. He realized, however, that he should not venture out until there were more people about, so lay on his stomach and watched the rain and tried to plan his day. One of the first things he must try and do was to sell his valuables, as he now only had a jar of jam left in stock and was already feeling peckish again.

After a long, long wait a few macintoshed children appeared on the beach, digging and running in and out of the sea as though it were a sunny day. A soaked dog, chasing sticks, hurtled in under Royston's hut and sent sand spraying into his eyes, but did not appear to notice him, though it frightened him. Soon after this the rain eased off and then stopped. More people arrived with deck-chairs and primus stoves. Royston escaped unnoticed from the hut, leaving the attaché case half-buried in sand – but he knew he could find it again. He took the chiming cigarette-box with him, wrapped in a piece of newspaper he found on the beach.

He did not have a successful morning. He got his cup of tea all right, and felt all the better for it; but he had forgotten that this was Saturday, and though it was a grey and inhospitable day the streets were full of slowly-moving crowds and the shops seemed only to sell buckets and spades and plastic windmills and were busy selling, not buying. He did go inside one shop whose window was stacked with ashtrays and fretwork, and he hung about in there in an agony of nervousness, but it was full of customers and nobody paid any attention to him, so eventually he crept miserably out again, his cigarette-box still unsold.

In the early afternoon he wandered into a public park and found a boy trying to balance on a motionless bicycle, so he showed him the box, and the boy said: 'Coo! Less 'ave a look. 'Ow much yer want for it?'

'Two bob,' said Royston.

'Coo! Did yer pinch it?'

'Yes.'

'Coo! 'Ere, Baz! Come over 'ere an' see wot this kid's pinched!'

So the other boy came over and said: 'Coo! Innit smashing! 'Ow much yer want for it?'

'Two bob.'

'Coo! Did you pinch it?'

'Yes.'

'Coo! 'Ere, Den! Come over 'ere an' see wot this kid's pinched!'

And so it went on, with more and more boys coming, and the

last ones were quite big lads, and eventually a sardonic youth in a blue suit flecked with gold pushed Royston over, took the box and went off with it, jeering, and most of the other boys departed rapidly on their bikes. Royston was swept with a wave of bitter despair, and fell to weeping uncontrollably. Presently one boy who had remained near him, looking embarrassed, came back and asked him what was the matter; and when Royston told him part of the story, the boy went home and fetched sixpence and a piece of cheese. He spent the money on some chips from the fish shop and a packet of Spangles and then wandered back towards the sea. He felt miserable and undecided, and did not dare creep back under the beach-hut, though that was what he felt like doing. His stomach felt unevenly distended and he discovered with horror that he had no penny for a lavatory; but he found a public one where one cubicle was labelled 'Free for Juveniles', so that was all right. He sat there for a long time with his cheek against the rough-cast wall, his eyes closed, occasionally shuddering.

Soon after five o'clock it began to rain again, but there were still a lot of people about, waiting for the pubs to open or queuing up at a coach rendezvous, wearing sodden paper hats. He did not dare to try and creep back under the beach-hut, because there were people sitting in it, so he found a shelter on the front and sat there for a long time, listening to the rain hissing into the sea. He was no longer thinking about the reasons for his being there; the problem was now one of simple survival. His stomach ached emptily. The thought of another night under the hut was unbearable. He was compelled to find shelter, warmth and food.

He stuck it out, hunched in a corner of the shelter, until the street-lights came on; then he got up stiffly and began to walk inland, looking for a house to break in to. He passed through the belt of mean streets and little houses which clustered behind the hotels, for burglary, which he now contemplated, was only associated in his mind with large houses. He trudged on, his wet shirt sticking to his back, occasional cars swishing past along the black and oily streets. Presently he came to an area of wider avenues, squares, crescents, trees and lilac-shaded gardens; he began to nose about cautiously, looking for a house where no lights showed.

After a long search – during which he became much more careless about concealment, and began talking to himself – he found a house, near the end of a crescent overlooking a small oval municipal shrubbery. It was a semi-detached house with a porch, shielded to some extent by a garden full of glistening bushes. He crept round by the side door and stood between the dustbins and the coal-bunker. Not a light showed anywhere. He tried the back door, but it was locked. He then noticed that the kitchen window was just ajar: not enough to get his hand in, but if he broke the glass, he could reach the catch. He got a piece of coal and gave the pane a sharp rap; the coal broke, but so did the glass, with an appalling crash. In his panic, he decided that he would be safer inside than out; he wrenched the window open and scrambled in over the sink, knocking a basin to the floor with a clatter; dropped to his hands and knees and gasped for breath.

No sound came from outside save the whisper of the rain and the faint flapping of the curtain, which now dangled out through the open window. He raised his head and cautiously looked about him; the kitchen was shadowy, but some of the grey shapes could be identified as furniture. On the other side of the door a clock ticked in the silence; and as it marked off each half-minute and there was no disturbance or alarm, he became quite confident. He found a box of matches on the gas-stove and lit some while he explored the larder. There he found two cold sausages and a remnant of apple-pie, which he ate, and a tin of condensed milk, which he opened and spooned up. Then he went off to look for some clothes, having some idea of lighting a fire and drying his own; every door was opened in a breath-catching moment, but he got around all the rooms, striking matches in each. On a ledge by the front door he found an insurance book with two half crowns lying on it, so he took them, and upstairs there was a little pile of threepenny bits on a mantelpiece, and he swept those, too, into his pocket. Of suitable clothes there were none, so he decided that one of the overcoats in the hall would do to wrap up in while his own clothes dried. He sauntered down the stairs, whistling softly, and in a burst of excitement and self-confidence took the last three stairs in a bound.

As his feet touched the hall floor, the front door was flung open and the lights came on.

He faced Nemesis with a curious sense of relief; he felt humiliated, too, at being caught, and sickened with sudden nervous tension, but on the whole was glad enough that all was over and now he only had to stand still and watch.

'How many of you?' barked the short man carrying the poker.

'Only me,' said Royston.

The man looked at him narrowly.

'All right,' he said at last. 'You stay by the door, Miss Mole, to show the police where we are. I can deal with this young man.'

Miss Mole, who was a plumpish grey-haired woman in a plastic mac, took up her position in the doorway whence she could keep one eye on Royston and one open for the police; but it was Royston who took up almost all her attention.

By the time the police arrived, huge men in streaming capes, fatigue had caught up with Royston and he was nearly out on his feet. He answered their questions patiently, and humbly showed them around the house where he'd been. He accepted without emotion the ride back to the police station in the car and the mug of tea from the friendly bald-domed sergeant who was in charge. Dimly he heard the policeman saying something about not being able to proceed save in the presence of the father, and then just as he was dozing off a sharp fresh young voice said: 'Sorry to interrupt, Sar'nt, the penny's only just dropped: isn't this the missing young person we had circularized this morning, wasn't that Beedman?'

'Let's have a look, then. Oh, ah. Believed to have proceeded by train to East Whixham, that's him. Ah. Oh, well, we'll ring up the home straight away, then.'

Royston was startled into wakefulness again. For more than twenty-four hours he had given no thought to his home at all – for him it had ceased to exist – and now he was wrenched back to realize and recapitulate all that had happened and what it would be like to go back there and why he was where he was, and he was still grappling with this rush of mental activity when the sergeant came in from the telephone room next door. Up to now the sergeant had been most fatherly and kind; now his voice had a much sharper edge to it: 'Well, boy: I'd like to know what you've been up to. I've been on the telephone to your parents and they won't have you back!'

6

THE Probation Officer for Francombe was an oldish man nearing retirement; he had started in Liverpool after the First World War, and his faded, kindly blue eyes had gazed with equanimity on a great many human beings since then.

Mr Beedman received him discourteously. 'I suppose you'd better come in.'

The Probation Officer was left alone to wipe his boots and to dart a quick, appraising glance round the hall. From the room to his left came a mutter of voices: 'Who the hell is it?'

'Somebody called Parkinson. Probation Officer or something.'

'Oh God! will it never end?'

Mr Beedman came back into the hall. 'Make it snappy, will you, the wife's not well.'

'Very good, sir. Now, your lad is to appear before the Whixham magistrates on Wednesday, I understand.'

'I know that. So what?'

'It's my job to make a brief report to the magistrates on the home circumstances of each lad.'

'Is that usual?'

'Oh yes, sir, part of the routine in these cases, I'm afraid.'

'You want to know my full name, age, and income, I suppose, and how much pocket money he gets, and how often I beat him?'

'Something along those lines, sir.'

'The police have already got all that. You're wasting your time.'

'Possibly, sir, but when I'm required to give evidence I like to check that my information is correct.'

'Then why the hell don't you check it with the police instead of coming here mucking up my evening? Anyway, I'm washing my hands of the whole affair; it's no longer my business.'

'How is that, sir?'

'Because I've had enough, that's how. Because I don't want to hear any more about it. Because when that boy removed himself out of my care and custody on Friday afternoon, whatever the hell he did after that was his affair, not mine.'

'I see, sir, yes, a very good argument. Very sensible.'

Mr Beedman was startled. He had been indulging in nothing but a moody roar and was surprised to find it accepted so earnestly. Nothing to fear from this bloke, evidently; just another down-trodden third-rater. He said, in a somewhat mollified tone: 'All right, take this down then: Gilbert Everard Beedman, age 49, Company director, income fifteen hundred plus; Christine Brenda Beedman, age 43, housewife.'

The Probation Officer was growing tired of standing and his fibrositis was giving him hell; he had one hundred and twenty-four cases on his books, he'd dropped everything to get here tonight, and he loathed night-driving. Nevertheless, he got everything down.

'M-h'm. Thanks. And Royston's your only child?'

'Yes,' said Mr Beedman, after a short pause.

'I mean, he's the only one living at home?'

'He doesn't live here,' said Mr Beedman.

'No, quite, but normally –'

'Normally he doesn't live here,' said Mr Beedman. 'Just get this, what's your name, Phillipson –'

'Parkinson.'

'All right, but just get this: when that boy walked out of this house on Friday – and he went of his own free will, there was no row or trouble, write that down – he walked right out of it: home, name, clothes, money, the lot. He chose not to belong here, so he doesn't belong here. He's finished.'

'Quite so, Mr Beedman, I realize how you must feel, but of course, the law says –'

'I know a little about the law, thank you. Listen: I'm a business man, and a good one; when I make a decision, it's a decision; when I say finished I mean finished – not finished this week back again next. Finished.'

'Yes, but –'

'The boy can go back where he came from.

'You mean –?'

'I mean he's not mine, he never was mine, and he never will be mine, and if I've now made myself clear you can leave it at that, can't you?'

The Probation Officer shifted his position painfully and looked about for something to lean against. He wanted nothing so much as to leave it at that, to get out of here and back to his own fireside, and yet he knew he'd turned up something that would have to be looked into. Fortunately, Mr Beedman's last outburst had fetched forth his wife.

'Can't you keep your voice down?'

Mr Beedman gave a disgusted snort and turned away. Parkinson summoned up another reserve of stamina and said smilingly: 'Mrs Beedman? My name is Parkinson, I'm a Probation Officer; I'm so sorry to trouble you this evening, but I have to make a report for the guidance of the magistrates when they come to deal with your boy.'

'I know.'

'Now, do I understand that you are actually foster-parents in this case?'

'Yes.'

'The boy is in the care of the County Council?'

'He's adopted.'

'Legally adopted?'

'Naturally.'

Parkinson rattled his pencil thoughtfully between his teeth. 'Does Royston know this?'

'Of course he doesn't.'

'Still thinks he's entitled to all this, I suppose,' said Mr Beedman. 'Well, he's got another think coming.'

'What were the circumstances of the adoption?'

'How do you mean? It was made at Chipham, when he was about six months old.'

'Oh, yes. No, I meant, was he – er – was it done through an Adoption Society?'

'No.'

'Did you know the mother yourself?'

54

'Yes.'

Parkinson waited hopefully, but nothing else came, so at last he sighed deeply and shut his notebook.

'Well, thank you, madam, I'm sure; and you, sir. You'll be attending at court, no doubt?'

'Catch me!' snarled Mr Beedman from the background.

'For God's sake, we haven't got to go, have we?'

'It would be advisable, madam: the magistrates can insist on your presence.'

'Are the magistrates going to pay expenses?' asked Mr Beedman sarcastically.

'Well, you'll have to go, Gilbert; I'm not going to a place like that and I certainly don't want to see Royston again. Where is he, by the way?'

'He's at Kings Lees, madam – the Remand Home, you know.'

Mrs Beedman gave a slight shudder. 'Will you take his clothes?' she asked.

'I'm afraid I shan't be seeing the boy, madam. My colleague Mr Browne handles that end.'

Mrs Beedman closed her eyes and massaged her forehead with the palm of her hand. 'All his belongings are packed up ready – I'd like them collected at the earliest possible moment. Will you please arrange it?'

'I'll see that's passed on, certainly, madam; and now I must take my leave. Good evening, and thank you.'

And Mr Parkinson bowed himself out along the drive and fitted himself carefully into the Ruby saloon he drove. 'Cor!' he exclaimed, as the car moved off: 'What a pair!' he said, as he changed up into third; and when he was in top he said to the passing hedgerows: 'Now, I bet he's her illegitimate. Poor little basket. What a life!'

He glanced at his watch – nearly eight; time for just one more visit; that blasted Pendry family, he supposed. Mr Parkinson sighed deeply and put Royston out of his mind. ...

Fifty miles away, another Probation Officer, a young fair-haired, rather nervous chap, had got hold of Mr Dunnet at the school.

'Royston Beedman?' mused Mr Dunnet, settling back in the tattered armchair and putting the tips of his fingers together. 'Nice lad, nice lad; I'm sorry to hear he's in trouble.'

'Breaking and entering, I understand,' said the Probation Officer.

'Dear me; foolish lad,' said Mr Dunnet. He had only a vague notion of what the words meant.

'Was he troublesome here, sir?'

'Not in the least. That's what I don't understand: whatever could have possessed the boy?'

'Would you say he was disturbed, or psychopathic in any way?'

'Oh, no; oh, no, no, nothing like that,' said the headmaster in a rather shocked voice, implying: we don't have that sort of thing *here*.

'How would you rate his ability? Have you his I.Q., by the way?'

'Ah, well, now, I am one of that not inconsiderable minority in this country which doubts the validity of the I.Q. as a guide to a boy's personality,' said the headmaster, in the pontifical tones he adopted when he was pretending to be a leading educationalist. 'But if you want my estimate – an entirely un-official estimate, mark you – I would say he was –' here he gazed at the ceiling for a moment '– ninety-three.'

The Probation Officer maintained his courteous expression as he thanked him and asked: 'Was he working up to that?'

'Oh, he was backward,' admitted Mr Dunnet. 'He'd been in quite a number of schools, I believe, which never helps. But he was working fairly well – occasionally he used to indulge in moodiness, but I believe he would have made the grade.'

'What was your impression of the boy's home?'

'Nothing untoward, I would say. Mind you, I hardly knew the parents – Beedman had only been with me for two terms, after all. But they paid promptly and Mr Beedman always strikes one as a competent, prosperous fellow.'

'H'm. Why did they send the boy here, sir, do you think?'

Weariness overcame the headmaster and made him say bit-terly: 'Oh, why do any of them send their boys here? Parents can't be bothered with 'em, I suppose; and we are not at all expensive. ...'

The Court House at East Whixham had been built just before the war and was a large, clean building with one wing used as police headquarters. In the other wing were the court rooms, waiting rooms, counsels' rooms, cashiers' and probation offices – all light, bright, and airy and smelling intensely of floor polish. The Juvenile Court area was separated from the main vestibule by a line of brass posts and chains.

At midday on Wednesday the Juvenile Court itself was completely silent, save for the measured tapping of the chairman's pencil. It was a highly polished room panelled with pale grey wood. By the door two policemen had fallen into the ruminative immobility of their profession, like two cart-horses in the noon sun. In the centre of the room sat Royston, again wearing the frayed shirt and too-tight trousers, looking small and lonely in the ocean of polished parquet. To his left, at a long table, sat a police inspector and the Clerk, both looking mournful; to his right sat Mr Browne, the Senior Probation Officer, moodily scanning his report. About two yards behind Royston sat Mrs Beedman, clad in a severe black suit and her mink wrap; her eyes were fixed on a spot on the floor a yard ahead and a little to one side, and there was an expression of intense distaste on her face. Her glance and her expression had not changed since she arrived, and her only word to the court so far had been: 'Nothing.'

At the back of the room, sitting uncomfortably side by side, were a short man, his tufty white eyebrows cocked alertly, and Miss Mole, whose expression was one of compassion.

Royston had been brought before the court on a charge of breaking and entering a dwelling-house. He had said yes, he'd done that, and the police evidence had been given in a rapid mutter by the inspector. When asked if he had anything to say, Royston had shaken his head; and to the same question, Mrs Beedman had said: 'Nothing.' Then the Home Circumstances Report had been laid before the magistrates by the Probation Officer and they had begun to read it in a silence broken only

57

by the tapping of the chairman's pencil. She was a heavily-built woman dressed in bright green and wearing spectacles with broad black frames and a hat with a tall feather in it. She tapped the pencil on the table, ran her fingers down to the point, reversed the pencil and repeated the process.

Presently the chairman raised her head with a sigh and gave Mrs Beedman a long, thoughtful and decidedly hostile stare. Then she said to the Clerk: 'I suppose we could compel the father to attend?'

'Yes, madam, you could, though I fear it would necessitate an adjournment till next week.'

'H'm. Perhaps not worth it; actions speak louder than words, I suppose.'

She frowned at the report again. 'Clear the court,' she said.

The two police cart-horses were galvanized into activity and everybody was ushered outside except the magistrates and their Clerk. The chairman leaned back heavily and sighed. 'Oh, these adoptions! They are worrying, you know; they do go abominably wrong.'

Her colleague grunted non-committally: he was thinking of the thousands of adoptions which turn out very well indeed.

'Well, anyway, this particular one's obviously gone on too long already. That's the problem, isn't it, not the offence itself?'

'Yes, I agree,' said her colleague. 'I think it probable that at the time the lad was simply acting out of sheer desperation.'

'I'm thinking of a Fit Person Order.'

'That might be appropriate, madam,' nodded the Clerk, 'but the only difficulty I envisage is that the local authority should be permitted to make representations before such an order is made, and, of course, no notice has been served upon them.'

'You mean we've got to adjourn? Send the boy back to the Remand Home?'

'Yes. Or you might consider making an Interim Order for twenty-eight days and then the boy could go to the Reception Home at Banns Cross for observation.'

The chairman gazed thoughtfully at her clerk and then said: 'No. I don't like all this messing to and fro. Clearly this boy needs help and needs it quickly; equally clearly the home is

58

absolutely u/s; and I'm not at all happy about his going back to the Remand Home for a further period of uncertainty and stress. What does this representation business mean – they can't refuse to have the boy, can they?'

'Oh, no,' said the Clerk. 'Even if they've protested strongly beforehand, the local authority cannot refuse to accept the Order. It's a matter of, oh, etiquette, I think; usually just so that a children's officer can be in attendance to take delivery of the child, as it were. Mr Ponto usually comes down from the Shire Hall.'

'Oh, yes, I know him. Nasty little man. So it would meet the case, would it, if we adjourn for half an hour so that this representative can get here? We could take this Pritch girl in the meantime.'

'I think that would be reasonable, madam.'

'I can't see that it makes much odds. After all, if the boy had been discovered on the beach before he committed this offence, the local authority would have had to find accommodation for him, probably, even if it were the middle of the night. So I can't see that we're treating them unfairly now.'

Her colleague had been listening silently all this time; he now nodded sagely, to put the seal on the decision, and the case was duly adjourned for half an hour. Mr Browne hurtled off to the telephone and Mrs Beedman gazed impatiently out of the vestibule window, beating her gloves disdainfully against the palm of her left hand.

A little later a breathless girl arrived from the Area Children's Office, and came into court. She had short crisp red hair and looked incredibly young to be representing a huge and wealthy County Council. The chairman nodded kindly to her and then said:

'Now, stand up, Royston. We have given a great deal of thought to your case and we have been very worried about you. We think you were probably feeling very unhappy and depressed at home, but, you know, however unhappy you may have felt, it was absolutely no excuse for you to go and do that very wrong and wicked thing you did do, getting into somebody else's house and doing that damage and trying to steal that money, and you must never, never do such a thing again. Will you promise me that?'

Royston made a jerky bob of the head and the chairman went on: 'Otherwise you'll be in very serious trouble indeed. Now, we also feel that there are too many difficulties in your own home at the moment for you to cope with, and in any case your parents say they will not have you there any more. So we are going to put you under the care of the County Council, and that means that you will get a fresh start and the chance to make good and put all this breaking and entering nonsense right behind you. There will be plenty of people to help you and advise you, so you try and listen to what they say and just jolly well see that you keep out of trouble in the future. Now, you go along off with this lady here, Royston, and don't let me ever see you in here again.'

The chairman finished with an imperious nod, and Royston found himself wafted out of the court. A cheery policeman engaged him in conversation; but he was watching his 'mother' stride down the vestibule away from him, without turning her head, still beating her gloves on the palm of her hand. She disappeared through the main entrance, and Royston felt dreadfully alone. He had no idea what had happened and had the notion that he was now to be kept in some dark and dusty cellar under the Council Offices.

Presently the young red-haired lady came out with several copies of a blue document, which she stowed in her handbag, and she gave him a cheery smile and said: 'Right, now, Royston. I am Miss Strachan, how do you do? We'll be on our way too, shall we?'

And then another voice, a rather timid voice, asked: 'Where will he be going, miss?' It was Miss Mole.

'He's going to the Reception Centre at Banns Cross.'

'Oh, yes. That's nice. And will he be properly looked after there, miss?'

'Yes, of course,' smiled the Child Care Officer.

'Good. Oh good. I pray God he will turn out a good lad. I'm sure he can be.'

Miss Strachan hurried Royston away from this unexpected

and not altogether welcome intruder whose standing she did not know, and they climbed into a small tourer outside and sped off.

Presently the Child Care Officer turned to Royston. 'I hope you'll like Banns Cross,' she said. 'Well, I'm sure you will. It's a biggish house, but at the moment there aren't many children there, so you'll find it quite peaceful.'

'Is it like the Remand Home?' ventured Royston.

'Oh, it's much nicer. Much nicer. But it's true it's something like the Remand Home, because you'll be there for just a month or two while we work out what's the best plan for you. You'll try and make friends with the staff and talk to them, won't you? because they can help you more if you tell them all about yourself.'

Royston did not take kindly to the idea of talking to all and sundry about his secret life, and he could not understand all this business about helping him. He didn't feel like a drowning man.

'Especially Mr Lloyd-Chamberlain: he's the warden of the Centre and awfully nice; he'll do his best to help you. He'll probably meet us, but then he usually gets one of the children to show a new arrival around and see him settled in, so you'll probably have your first real talk with him tomorrow.'

Royston listened politely to all this, but it meant very little to him. However, it was pleasant to feel the wind whistling through his hair as they sped through a maze of narrow lanes, and he was sorry when at last they roared into the courtyard of a large old house and a fresh wave of apprehension flooded over him.

Mr Lloyd-Chamberlain did meet them, and was very pleasant. 'How do you do, Royston? Very nice to have you here, come along in. Now, we must find somebody to show you all round, mustn't we, see you settled in. Ah, here's just the fellow! Come and meet Royston.'

The boy emerged from the shadows at the back of the huge entrance-hall and came up to them.

'Coo!' cried Royston. 'Hallo, Tod!'

7

ROYSTON soon got used to the daily round at the Reception Centre, and did what was required of him without either accepting or challenging the necessity of it. He had, of course, been in other residential establishments and knew how to make a rough-and-ready adjustment to the life, and also he knew that he was not going to live in this particular one for very long. It was just another resting place, and had another set of adults moving about in it with whom he needed to make only the most superficial contact. He found out pretty quickly that this lot weren't a bad lot, and they meant well, he supposed; after that he occupied his time as pleasantly as he could.

It wasn't a bad place to be in by any means, especially after the Remand Home. Kings Lees had not been a harsh place, but it had been quite bleak – there was little furniture, the routine was rigid and closely supervised, and you could never be alone. The boys, who ranged in age from eight to sixteen, were dressed in khaki shirts and shorts and close haircuts; the staff were all male, and they regarded their charges 'as a tired man looks at flies'. Many of the boys had never been away from home before, and had been led to believe that the Remand Home was something horrific; they were thus agreeably surprised when they found themselves not merely surviving but gaining a sense of well-being from the early-to-bed, early-to-rise régime. Royston found the whole place regrettable.

Banns Cross at least set out to be a *home* : there were carpets in most of the rooms, you could beetle about, unsupervised, in the grounds, and the staff, mostly female, bustling round on tasks that were recognizably domestic even if on a large scale, did create a different sort of atmosphere. You had to make your bed every morning, and bumper the bedroom lino, and you might be on potatoes, or on washing up, or on laying the dining tables, but then you got that in any residential place; and you could wander out to the shops or the pictures on a Saturday, or go train-spotting if you wanted, or make a tree house, or muck about round the paddling pool or sit playing Monopoly. It wasn't too bad, time could be made to pass; it was just utterly boring, that was all.

There were not many children in the Centre at that time, and since some of these were toddlers and some haughty teen-age girls, Royston did not have much choice of companions. In the senior boys' bedroom were only Tod and himself; Pfeiffer, an embittered Nazi youth who had not been long in England, and Billy Williams, a slouch-mouthed inane boy who was on holiday from a school for the sub-normal. Tod and Royston were thus thrown together to some extent, although Royston often felt like being on his own for perhaps an hour or two, and Tod was frequently off on some mysterious lone-wolf activity. Royston came, somewhat reluctantly, to admire the older boy for his competence: it was Tod who knew how to carry extra slices of bread up to the dormitory tucked inside his shirt, who knew how to get apples from the neighbouring orchard, and who knew the place behind the mattress-store where they could smoke. They got cigarettes by robbing the little ones in the Centre, using a form of Protection Racket: on Sundays, after visitors had been, leaving gifts, it was usually possible to collect a fair amount of pocket-money from them before the Warden got told of it. Any recalcitrant child was usually beaten up by Pfeiffer, who was not in the racket but whom Tod could easily goad by quoting fictitious insults. Billy Williams, who was heavily in debt to Tod from the first day of his holiday, was used for buying the cigarettes or occasionally for taking the rap.

Although Royston appreciated, even enjoyed, sharing this business with Tod, there were some aspects of the older boy's character that he did not like. He never, for instance, recognized in Tod any sense of loyalty for anybody; he himself would have stood by Tod, if necessary, and even sacrificed himself to authority, but he was pretty sure that Tod would throw him to the wolves without giving it a thought. Again, Tod loved upsetting or worrying him with tall autobiographical stories, never wholly

63

unbelievable and full of cruel or disgusting episodes – people's eyes getting torn out by spikes, for instance. And finally, Tod was preoccupied with sex; almost every phrase and remark made by anybody was sniggered over, and Royston had to listen to detailed accounts of Tod's exploits. He came to regard Tod with mingled admiration and revulsion.

One day, when they were having a smoke before dinner, Tod said: 'Committee day today.'

'What's that?'

'Lots of ole bags and geezers come an' sit round a big table in the Quiet Room and decide wot they're goin' to do wiv us,' said Tod.

'What sort of thing?'

'Where they're goin' to send us to next.'

'Do we have to go to Committee?'

'No; daft! They never arsk us wot we want. We can find out later on, like, if we can get 'old of ole Chamber-Pot's big book.'

'Do they sometimes decide to let somebody stay here?'

'Ooh no. Everybody's got to be moved on. They'll send us somewhere; probably miles away.'

A feeling of uncertainty and depression suddenly swept over Royston. . . .

Inside the Quiet Room the case conference got rapidly down to work. As there were not many children in the Centre, and many of these were regular visitors on holiday from special schools, about whom discussions had little point, the meeting was able to give more time to the two new boys.

'Well, now, let's have a look at Beedman,' said the Children's Officer. 'Warden?'

'He's settled down very well,' said Mr Lloyd-Chamberlain. 'Remarkably well, considering what he must have been through at home.'

'Parents haven't been in contact, I suppose?'

'No, not a word. Oh, a parcel of clothing arrived, presumably from the mother, but there was no letter inside.'

'We had a stinking letter from the father, madam, about his assessment for contributions,' said Mr Ponto, the Administrative

Officer. 'Seemed to think he needn't pay as he wasn't the boy's father. We are applying for a Justices' Order against him.'

'Good,' said the Children's Officer. She didn't like men much. 'Has the boy opened up yet about what happened?'

'No; he's being very cagey,' said the Warden. 'We've got one or two clues, of course; for instance, the other day I had occasion to have all the boys on the mat – a bit of jiggery-pokery over pocket-money, it was. Billy Williams was at the bottom of it – but Royston went as white as a sheet, and when I stood up at one point he absolutely flinched away. I think he's been beaten; more than once, I would guess.'

'Is he loyal to his parents?'

'Difficult to say, he talks so little. He's not actively rejecting them, at any rate.'

'Can you help us on that at all, Dr Maclaren?'

The psychiatrist jerked forward out of his stupor and removed his spectacles.

'I'm afraid I've not seen this particular laddie, Miss Kelpie, having been on leave myself, d'ye see,' he said. 'He was, however, seen by one of the Educational Psychologists, Mrs Carfax. I have her report here.'

He replaced his spectacles, sorted through the files in front of him and then said: 'No: I seem to have brought the wrong files, these are all the Kings Lees cases. However, I can give you the gist of her report, which was that Royston is of average intelligence though retarded in the basic subjects and more successful in tests involving manual dexterity. He cooperated quite well, responded to praise and showed some capacity to relate. Mrs Carfax felt that he was not, shall we say, a priority case for full diagnostic examination. I think we can say, with many reservations of course, that the adoption probably went fairly well in its early stages at least: the boy must, I think, have experienced a loving relationship during the danger period before six.'

'Of course, he's adopted. I'd forgotten that,' said the Children's Officer. 'Does he know he is?'

'No,' said Mr Lloyd-Chamberlain.

'We shall have to break it to him, then. Or shall we, Doctor?'

But the psychiatrist fell into deep thought and made no reply.

'There is a suggestion in the probation report, excuse my interrupting,' said the Matron, 'that Royston may be the illegitimate son of Mrs Beedman, born before marriage. I wonder if that would account for the fact that things apparently went all right in early years; and that later, perhaps, he became a threat to the marriage?'

'Now, that's very ingenious, Mrs Lloyd-Chamberlain,' said Dr Maclaren. 'I wouldn't go so far as to say that was definitely a causative factor, but it could be so, certainly it could be so.'

'Is there not – I mean, is there a chance of rehabilitating that home?' asked a scholarly child-care officer with a horsey face.

'Precious little on the evidence, I think,' said the Children's Officer. 'Old Parky put in a damning report; I know he's getting a bit old and past it, but his assessments are still pretty shrewd. Besides, you know, the kid bolted once before – Mr Ponto found a police report on him we'd forgotten all about, which doesn't give much encouragement.'

'I'd say there was a chance of rehabilitation,' said Dr Maclaren. 'Especially if the woman would accept help; but it would be a long job, and I would say that a return home at this early stage is definitely contra-indicated.'

'It's the father who's the trouble, madam, surely; he's a stinker,' said Mr Ponto.

'One of the difficulties in this case, I feel,' said the Chief Welfare Officer, 'is that these parents are of a cultural level that we don't often come across: I mean, most of our parents accept welfare officers and probation officers as quite normal encumbrances, but these people think it's disgraceful that any such lowly form of life should be seen on their doorstep. It's going to take one officer a long, long time even to get accepted.'

'Whose area is the home in?' asked the Children's Officer.

'Horniman's.'

'Oh lord! No, she won't do. Well, my own inclination is to write off the parents completely; although I appreciate what you said just now, Dr Maclaren. I think this is an adoption that should never have happened; it hasn't shown any staying power and I think it's best if we cancel it and all start again – it's too complicated any other way. Yes, well now. Any relatives, by the way?'

There was a blank silence.

'Oh, I should have mentioned before, I'm sorry,' said Mr Lloyd-Chamberlain. 'There was a rather mysterious telephone call from East Whixham, a woman called Mole, Miss Mole, I think it was, inquiring about Royston. I couldn't quite make out who she was, but I think she was somebody he met there when he was on the loose.'

'Did the boy know her?'

'No, he'd never heard of her.'

'Somebody who'd read the case in the papers, I suppose, and wanted to adopt him,' said the Children's Officer. 'We can't have every Tom, Dick, and Harry poking a nose into this, it's too delicate a matter. So, no relatives. What about boarding-out?'

But there was a chorus of dissent to this.

'I think there are strong objections to boarding out any child over the age of six,' said Dr Maclaren.

'He's suffered too much from close relationships, he needs a period of reduced intensity,' said Matron.

'He needs a further period of study, I feel; he's been very cagey here,' said Mr Lloyd-Chamberlain.

'We haven't got any foster-homes for a boy of this age,' said the Chief Welfare Officer.

'Fair enough.' The Children's Officer shrugged. 'It means a long-stay Home, then. We're very hard-pressed for places – what is the position, Ponto?'

'We have precious few, madam. For a boy of this age, I think the only place is at Hawthorn Hill.'

'Yes. Any comment, Doctor?'

'Who's in charge there?'

'The Woodingtons.'

'Oh aye; yes. Good as anywhere.'

'Good.' The Children's Officer made a note on the file. 'Hawthorn Hill it is; Miss Strachan, you brought him in. Would you arrange the transfer?'

'Yes, Miss Kelpie.'

'Good. Now, then: Tod.'

There was a sense of relaxation round the table: stretching of legs, some wry grins, and suppressed chuckles. This was a different kettle of fish – they knew they couldn't do much about Tod.

'Warden?'

'Nothing further to add, Miss Kelpie. I think he's best described as an incorrigible rogue; there's something likeable about him, a superficial air of engaging mischief, but underneath I'm afraid he's as cold and slippery as a snake.'

'Snakes aren't, as a matter of fact; but I know what you mean, Doctor. You were considering ascertaining him as maladjusted and trying to get him into a special school. Is that advisable?'

'Well, of course, most children would benefit from special education; but in this case – well, for one thing I think he's too old now for placement, and for another thing I can't honestly see that this boy requires special *educational* treatment. He's a mean, vicious, narcissistic type of boy, not a psychopath, I believe, but I think his behaviour is likely to be somewhat anti-social, self-seeking, aggressive, maybe even sadistic.'

'Quite an advertisement for the Department, in fact. Nothing from the foster-mother, I suppose? One could hardly expect it.'

'No.'

'What did go wrong there? I wasn't in on it,' said the Chief Welfare Officer.

'Oh, there'd been complaints for years, you know – dishonesty, late nights, rudeness, and threats. It finally broke down when the foster-mother took his pocket money to pay for some damage, and Tod went round to all the neighbours spreading the story that she was a heavy drinker and he had to undress her and put her to bed every night.'

'Endearing character, isn't he!'

'He's well over thirteen, I see, so I suppose all we can do is park him somewhere for the next eighteen months and think perhaps in terms of a working boys' hostel. Doctor?'

'I can't see what else you can do. If you've got a choice I'd like to see him with Mr Wardle at St Agnes House: he did very well with that Prince boy.'

'I'm afraid, madam, that there's no vacancy at St Agnes,' said Mr Ponto. 'There may be one at Christmas.'

'Goodness, we don't want to wait till Christmas, do we, Warden?'

'Well, frankly, Miss Kelpie, I'm sorry, but I'd like to see the boy out of here. He's got to know all the ropes, you see; he'd be Warden if I didn't crack down on him. He exerts such an influence on the newcomers, that's the trouble here. I hate myself for passing a problem on to my colleagues, but I do feel that perhaps this boy may do less damage in their settled groups than he could do here.'

'H'm. What can we do, Ponto?'

'Well, again I'm afraid it comes down to Hawthorn Hill, madam; they're the only Home with vacancies.'

'Oh dear, oh dear, oh dear,' said Mr Lloyd-Chamberlain. 'I don't like the influence Tod is exercising over Beedman, and I had rather hoped they could be separated.'

'Are they very thick?'

'Well – they do go around together a lot, but it is true, of course, that they're the only two in the boys' group who would. I mean, Williams is awfully dim and nobody likes Pfeiffer, so that Royston and Archibald have been more or less thrown together.'

'They'll have a wider choice of companions at Hawthorn Hill and so they may drift apart again,' observed Matron. 'I can't see that they have much in common really – they're as different as chalk from cheese.'

'Well, I can't see what else we can do,' said Miss Kelpie. 'I think we shall have to take the risk and send them together, and then just hope that the friendship breaks up later. After all, there's not long to go before Tod leaves us and there's over a year's difference in their ages, anyway. Yes. That's all we can do, I think.'

And so it was duly written down as the Conference conclusion that Tod and Royston should travel together, with Miss Strachan, to the mixed Home – boys and girls – at Bernards Green.

But by the time the Conference finished, both Royston and Tod had absconded.

8

ROYSTON'S feelings of uncertainty and depression persisted until lunch-time and became even more intense afterwards when the Committee cars began to arrive. He became more and more restless, and began to feel that it was unbearable to remain in the place while unknown wayward giants played dice for his future. Even the sophisticated Tod seemed to feel equally anxious and insecure, and it was with very few words exchanged that, by mutual consent, the two boys dodged the housefather on duty and broke out of bounds. They did not, in the first place, intend a serious absconsion.

They got on to the main road leading to town and the further they walked from the Reception Centre the lighter grew their spirits. They had no money with them and were at a loss for something to do, as they felt that having actually broken out of the Home they ought to be indulging in dare-devil feats of some sort. They turned off the road and spent some time in the children's playground; Tod stationed himself under the slide and gazed upwards at the knickers of the little girls climbing the ladder. Royston thought this a fatuous occupation, so he went over to the drinking-fountain and performed some squirting exercises.

It was some time before Tod realized that he had attracted the attention of a suspicious mother and beat a retreat. The two boys continued to mooch into town and had passed the Post Office and the traffic lights when Tod suddenly spied a familiar shop-front ahead and stopped.

' 'Ere!' he said. 'Let's 'ave a go in there.'

'How do you mean?'

'Pinchin'. You believe in pinchin', don't yer?'

Royston still found this a trick question. He was, these days, rather more strongly attracted to the idea of stealing, but at the same time the stern words of the magistrates had quite impressed him and he did not want to go to court again.

'Gah! Windy!'

'I'm not!' said Royston warmly. 'Anyway it's all very well for you – you haven't been in trouble before. I have, and I don't want to get in any more.'

'Orlright, then,' said Tod. 'You don't need to do any pinchin'. I'll do the pinchin'. I tole yer I was a good pincher, didn't I? You can watch. You can 'elp if you like.'

'How?'

'You get the ole girl's attention – get 'er up the other end of the counter. Go on, you go in first.'

So Royston went ahead into the shop, and as the stationery counter was nearest to the door, he went up to the far end and began turning over diaries and stamp albums. He was looking rather furtive and the assistant moved along with him to keep a watch on him. He saw Tod come up to the lower end of the counter and lean his folded arms on it while pretending to gaze at pen-and-pencil sets; hidden by the folded arms his fingers were busy plucking up and concealing anything he could touch. Royston began to feel exultant. He asked the assistant if she had a stamp album for British Empire issues only, and this confused her and made her rummage in her stock.

Suddenly there was a terrible commotion – a blue-overalled supervisor had swooped on Tod. The boy instinctively ducked and wheeled, escaped from her clutches and charged for the door, dropping two pencils and a packet of rubber bands and colliding violently with a short woman in black. The supervisor chased after him. Royston, panic-stricken, also began to run and the next moment was caught by the floor-walker, who cried: 'He's in it too!' Royston's instant denial was succeeded, to his horror, by a tremendous blush that turned his whole face and neck crimson. Tod got through the door and made good his escape.

'What are you boys doing? You wretched boys, we've had quite enough trouble with you!' cried the floor-walker in a high, lisping voice. 'You'd better come with me and see the manager.'

Royston found himself walked ignominiously through the staff door and into a stone corridor piled with cardboard boxes. They went up some stairs and into the manager's office, next to the canteen. Royston was halted in front of the manager's desk; he lowered his head sullenly and clasped his hands behind him.

The manager was a dispirited-looking fellow with glasses, who had been half-way through a cup of tea. He listened to the floor-walker's story in silence; he was mainly concerned with memorizing the boy's face, so that they could all be on their guard if Royston came into the store again. When the story was finished he said wearily: 'You're a very silly boy. Aren't you? Eh? You're just like all the other silly boys who come in here trying to knock things off, as you call it. Silly, that's what you are. You think we're soft, don't you, because we never prosecute anybody? We're not soft, you know. We know all about you. We could get you in big trouble if we wanted. Big trouble. Don't you forget it. Now don't you ever come in this shop again unless you've got your dad or your mum with you. Understand? Otherwise you'll get turned out straight away. Understand?'

Royston was dismissed; and with a sad shake of his head the manager returned to his tea. Royston was taken to the side door of the shop and coldly seen off. He marched up the street feeling furious and decided to visit the public lavatory by the housing office. Tod was there.

'You blooming fool, Tod!'

'Whassa matter wiv yer? Jus' cos you was too blooming slow –'

'What did you want to get copped for? You blooming fool! I wasn't doing anything and then I go and get copped for doing nothing!'

'Gah, you're feeble!'

'I'm not! What did you run off for and leave me to get in all the trouble? That's not blooming fair.'

'Wot, you think I oughter've come back and give meself up? Don't talk daft!'

'I'm not daft!'

'You are daft. Daft fool!'

'Daft yourself!'

'I got two pens, anyway,' said Tod, showing them. 'That's not so daft, is it? You didn't get nothin'!'

Royston felt extremely disgruntled. Then another thought struck him. 'Anyway, thanks to you I can't go back to the Home now.'

'Why not?'

'I've already been in court once, and they said I'd be in serious trouble if I went again.'

'Gah! They never take yer to court.'

'How do you know? I bet they do. Anyway they took my name and address, and they'll probably tell the police. The police can take you to court. And they will you, too. You and your blooming daft pens.'

Tod was silent. For no other reason than sheer blind luck, he had never been prosecuted himself, and he recognized that to some extent Royston was the legal expert of the partnership. After a long pause he said: 'Wot we goin' to do?'

Royston shrugged. 'I dunno. I don't fancy going back there just to get in trouble.'

'Did you give yer *real* name and address?' asked Tod suddenly.

'Yes.'

'You daft thing! I tole you you was feeble!'

Royston had no reply to this: he saw that he could very easily have managed things better.

The two boys emerged into the street and drifted around aimlessly. Near the Odeon they had a stroke of luck: they sold the two pens for a shilling to a boy in a grammar school blazer, and with the money they bought chips. It was this that decided them not to go back and face an alarming future. They resolved to make for the railway-line.

Mr Lloyd-Chamberlain gave them till nine o'clock and then reported them as missing. He had mildly rebuked the housefather – actually he had thought the man very feeble, but he dared not offend him in case he left and made the staff shorthanded again. Apart from this there wasn't much to be done about absconders, except adopt a philosophical attitude. One hoped, at first, that hunger and discomfort would bring them back; one occasionally, if it were a fine evening, took a drive round the lanes to see if there were any sign. Otherwise one waited till dark and then informed the police. Mr Lloyd-Chamberlain gave the details over the telephone – colour of hair, colour of eyes, clothing, distinguishing marks – and then settled down with a book, hoping that the runaways would be found not too far away and not too late at night, because he'd have to go and collect them.

At a quarter to ten the telephone rang. 'Good!' thought the Warden, as he went to pick it up. 'Not too far, not too late.'

'Is that Banns Cross 200?'

'Yes.'

'Can I speak to the Superintendent?'

'This is the Warden speaking.' Mr Lloyd-Chamberlain scowled at the telephone – this didn't sound like a policewoman. 'Who is that?'

'This is Miss Mole speaking; Miss Mole of East Whixham.'

Mr Lloyd-Chamberlain made an impatient strangled noise: fancy blocking up the telephone at a time like this!

'I'm ever so sorry to ring up so late like this,' said Miss Mole. 'Only I've got an unexpected day off tomorrow, and I wondered if I could p'raps come over and see Royston?'

There was only the shortest of pauses.

'I'm afraid it would be most inconvenient, madam,' said Mr Lloyd-Chamberlain coldly. Tom, Dick and Harry poking their noses in! 'Very inconvenient indeed!'

'Oh dear. Only you see I never get a Saturday off and I thought –'

'I'm sorry.' Get off this line, curse you!

'Do you know when I could p'raps see him?'

'That is entirely a matter for the Children's Officer, madam. I must point out that Royston was placed here by order of a Court of Law, and it is most unusual for the Children's Officer to allow access to the children at all.'

'Oh dear. I didn't know. Oh dear, I am sorry –'

'That is the position, and now –'

'I wouldn't have rung if I'd –'

'Quite; and now good –'

'I'm ever so sorry.'

'Good night, Miss Mole.'

'Only you don't mind my –?'

'Good night.'

And Mr Lloyd-Chamberlain replaced the receiver, hoping that the police had not been fuming over the engaged line.

By this time Royston and Tod had clambered down a cutting on to the railway-line and were moving cautiously over the ballast. They were finding the evening unexpectedly cold; they were also feeling hungry and rather bored. They had some idea of swinging themselves on to a passing goods train and travelling to God knew what exciting place; but not a single train had passed yet. They came to a signal, and Tod clambered up the ladder into the windy dark and tried to sabotage the mechanism, but he could not. They tried balancing on the lines, and springing from sleeper to sleeper; they put some stones on the line, and almost immediately a train rumbled by and crushed the stones with a great crunching. Tod was thrilled.

'A bloke was telling me a good trick,' he said. 'You put a 'apenny on the line and a train comes along and presses it out, like till it's as big as a penny, an' then you can put it in the bubblegum machine.'

Royston was not very interested. 'Come on!' he said. Tod skipped down the track like a goat; he was enjoying this novel experience. Royston, however, veteran now of three nocturnal expeditions, knew that without much more delay they must find shelter and some rest, ready for the following day. He was worried about food, too: he knew that hunger had driven him into trouble last time.

A quarter of a mile down the track they came to a siding, and on the siding stood four railway wagons, each covered with a tarpaulin. Here, obviously, was the solution to the shelter problem; they hastened over the tracks and clambered up the massive side of the end wagon. Under the tarpaulin they immediately felt warmer. The air smelt excitingly tarry and the floor of the wagon seemed to be covered with coal dust. It was a splendid den and Tod got quite excited.

'Shan't be long now, eh? Right away, guard!' he called, whistling sharply.

'Shut up, Tod, you blooming idiot!' hissed Royston.

'Mind the doors now, please!'

'Shut up you bloody fool!'

'The train now standing at Platform Two –' and Tod went on to give a list of fictitious station names, closely connected with the human digestive system. Royston buried his head in his arms. However, nobody came near the wagons and Tod slowly subsided. He began telling some dirty jokes of a singularly unlovely kind, laughing and sniggering away to himself till the wagon creaked and shook beneath him. Royston paid no heed at all; he was working on a private problem. He believed – as Tod also believed – that the wagon they were in was part of a train, and that the train would presently rumble off through the night. Where would he go? What would he do? What did he want? What *was* he?

Tod was beginning to settle down. Royston lay on his back, arms folded under his head, gazing up through a slit in the tarpaulin at a single bright star, and listened to the older boy swearing and chuckling and shifting about as he tried to get comfortable.

Presently Tod yawned mightily and said: 'Ah, well. Wot a flippin' life! Wonder where we'll be when we wake up, eh?'

'Mm,' said Royston, thoughtfully.

There was a pause.

'Tod?'

'Yer?'

'What happened to your mother?'

'I dunno.'

'Is she dead?'

'Naow! I dunno. Oo cares?'

'Don't you mind?'

'Naow! Not worth botherin' about. They're no bloody good to yer, women aren't.'

There was another pause.

'You gotta mother, Roy?'

'No,' said Royston, with an effort.

There was another short pause. Tod was shifting about, muttering crossly.

'Tod?'

'Wot now?'

'Do you remember, when we were talking together at Francombe, you told me to find my birth certificate?'

'Did I? I say lots o' things.'

'What did you find on yours?'

'Dunno. My mother wasn't married, I found that, 'cos there was just a line instead of Dad's name.'

Royston paused again and asked cautiously: 'Did you ever want to find out who your father was?'

'There's a bastard bit o' coal down my shirt. Come on out!' Tod was evidently playing for time, for presently he said: 'Yer. I did think of it.'

'How would you find him?'

'I'd find my mother first and I'd get 'er to tell. She would tell, too. I'd torture 'er till she told. Yes. Prob'ly I'd torture her anyway.'

This did not sound promising. Royston said: 'Supposing I wanted to find – well, my real mother – what do you think I should do?'

'Don't bloody well bother, mate. Wot's the use? You wanna forget all that caper. You look after number one, that's the thing for us bastards.'

'I only said supposing.'

Unexpectedly this appealed to Tod; there was some element of fantasy, of derring-do, in it.

'Well – you gotta grow bigger first of all – you can move about more then, those blooming coppers always stop yer when yer little. And then after that I s'pose you – where do you come from, anyway?'

Royston told him the story of the adoption and of how it had all turned out.

'Well, when you're big, as big as me, like, you could get 'old of them Francombe people and torture them till they told. They know where you came from all right, 'course they do. That's wot I'd do, torture 'em.'

This was a fantasy that Royston could not indulge in. 'Chipham,' he said. 'That's where it was done. I might find her there.'

'Don't you bloody bother. Women are no good to yer. Women are only good for one thing.'

These were the last words Royston heard before he drifted into sleep. . . .

An early-morning lengthman hauled them both out at dawn, filthy, bleary-eyed and shivering. The wagons had not moved; they were still in the same siding. Royston and Tod were taken along the track to the nearest station and the police were called by a disgusted clerk. The policemen were quite kind; the boys were given a cup of tea and a wash in a strangely dreamlike ablutions-room, full of policemen in shirt-sleeves, shaving. Then they were told to wait for Mr Lloyd-Chamberlain.

Both boys had suddenly descended in their own estimation from fully-grown adventurers to naughty little boys. Even in their cold and bleary state they needed to do something about this. They began sniggering privately at the policemen and inventing foolish sexual jokes about them. Then they began imagining their own triumphal return to Banns Cross.

'They won't know wot to do wiv us now, mate!' crowed Tod. 'We got them licked now; they won't know 'ow to 'old us, not now!'

'Do what we like; walk out when we choose!'

'S'right. Big stuff. See if we care! Huh!'

It was quite shocking to them when they were collected, bathed and sent over to Hawthorn Hill without anyone taking a bit of notice of them.

9

Miss Mole emerged cautiously from the shop at about a quarter to ten and walked down to the town centre. She was clutching her handbag so tightly that her knuckles were white, and all sorts of fears chased round in her mind – that someone would snatch her bag, that it would fall open without her noticing, that she would have a heart attack. The first thought would make her hurry for some distance; the second and third brought her up short and made her dawdle. This uncertain scouts' pace got her to the bank five minutes before the doors opened and she had to hang about outside in agony, feeling that an ironic fate would probably cheat her even now.

However, the doors opened and she got in. She had very rarely been in a bank before and felt shy. She went to the cashier nearest the door and told him her business in a timid mutter. He said he thought she ought to see the manager, and showed her into a large box, all mahogany and frosted glass, in a corner of the bank.

'My name is Forrest,' said the manager, shaking hands warmly. 'Do sit down, won't you?'

'Thank you. My name is Mole – er, Miss Constance Mole. Mr Stringer advised me to come and see you.'

'Oh, yes. I know Mr Stringer very well.'

'Yes,' said Miss Mole. She looked down at her hands, which were still clutching her handbag. 'The fact is,' she said, 'well, you see, very unexpectedly, I've come into some money and I thought you'd better look after it for me.' She swallowed; she felt parched. 'Here it is.'

She pushed the little mauve slip across the table and watched him pick it up with mingled feelings of relief that he'd got it, and terror that he handled it so carelessly. A puff of wind – a spark from the fire –!

Mr Forrest looked at her over his spectacles.

'Twelve thousand pounds? My dear Miss Mole, what have you been doing? Is this a pools win?'

'Ooh, no. No, it's a legacy, as a matter of fact: my brother.'

'Oh dear; that's rather a sad way for money to come to one.'

'Well – yes,' said Miss Mole, 'only you see Horry's been abroad for so long, and I've seen so little of him anyway, that – well, anyway, I've got over that part of it. I've known for a long time about the will and that, I just had no idea it was so much – oh, dear, I'm sorry, Mr Forrest, you don't want to hear all this.' Miss Mole became pink with confusion.

'But I do, Miss Mole, please! I really do!' said the manager. He was indeed very interested; as he used to tell the chaps at Rotary lunches, his hobby was 'the study of human nature'. 'Do tell me more. Your brother was married?'

'Oh, no. Just like me; neither of us was lucky enough. I'm the only relative Horry's got. Do you reelly want to know about us, Mr Forrest?'

'Indeed, yes.'

'Well: we were the only children in our family and Horry was the clever one, y'see; at least, so it turned out, though we never realized how clever, because when he left school he only went into the building trade, and didn't do all that well at that.'

Mr Forrest went on nodding his head and making encouraging little grunts.

'Well, then Horry went abroad on a construction job, to Kenya it was first of all, but then he went to Rhodesia and then Ceylon and after that, well, I reelly don't know where he went, all over, doing these construction jobs. He came home for Mum's funeral, and he was just the same old Horry, quiet and rather worried-looking, you know; and I was supposed to be going out to join him in 1939, only the war came. So I only actually saw him the once, y'see, and I had no idea, till just now, that for ages he'd been actually, well, the boss in his own little line! Incredible, I think it is.'

'Didn't you get any clue from his letters?' asked Mr Forrest.

'Well, we only wrote to each other at Christmas,' confessed

Miss Mole, 'and I'm blessed if Horry's letters were worth getting even then. D'you know, Mr Forrest, in spite of all that money and all that getting-on, I don't think Horry ever did learn to write letters very well.'

'I think that's a wonderful story, Miss Mole,' Mr Forrest said smilingly, 'and I think you've been very fortunate in your brother. And now the point is that you want us to look after the money, don't you? Now, what are your plans?'

Miss Mole went pink again and looked rather wildly round the office.

'Do I have to tell you that?' she asked.

'Why, no, Miss Mole, not if you don't wish to,' replied the manager, who was puzzled at first and then leapt to the conclusion that there was a man in this somewhere. 'I only asked in the most general terms so that I might advise you about investing the money; for instance, whether you will want to spend a small lump sum on some immediate necessity and invest the remainder to yield an income.

Miss Mole calmed down a little and said: 'I'm sorry; I didn't wish to be mysterious, Mr Forrest, only, well, you see, I *do* know what I want to try and do only I reelly haven't got things sorted out yet and anyway it's all a bit vague. Only what I thought, well, sort of roughly was that I'd like to put most of this money in an investment, y'see, and I'd go on working at the shop, only half-time, y'see, seeing that I wouldn't reelly know what to do with myself if I didn't do that, at any rate till my other what's-it comes off, if it does. Only what I would like to get, if I could, is a nice little bungalow, somewhere like Whix Park. I've lived in one room for a great many years, y'see,' she finished, rather wistfully.

Mr Forrest thought she sounded fairly sensible on the whole, except for this occasional evasive coyness which seemed a bit ominous. He talked at some length about different forms of investment and suggested that she spread her capital between them; he explained about security and interest, and about current and deposit accounts; and then at the end he asked: 'Might I inquire, Miss Mole, how many people here know of your good fortune?'

'Ooh, only you, Mr Forrest, and I did tell Mr Stringer at the shop.'

'Yes. You see, Miss Mole – I'm sure I don't really need to tell you this – but East Whixham is a funny place. There are a number of moneyed people, some elderly, some widowed, who have come here to live in retirement; and there are a number of rather sharp characters who cast a greedy eye on the money. You read the papers, of course: you know about the smooth doctors and nurses, the rather dramatic spiritualists, the fake inventors, and so on. Now, I can see that you're a very sensible woman, Miss Mole, but the point is that these people are extremely clever, extremely clever. I do give you this advice, Miss Mole, better keep quiet about what's happened and particularly keep quiet about the amount involved. Will you?'

'Yes, of course, Mr Forrest, thanks for telling me.'

'I realize what a great temptation it must be to blurt out the news to everybody,' said the student of human nature. 'Still – oh well, so long as you know what you're doing.'

'I don't know that I know just *what* I'm doing,' said Miss Mole, with another evasive glance. 'But anyway I know what I want to try and do.' And with that, and some pleasantries, she took her leave.

Mr Forrest need not have worried all that much. It was not a man who was occupying her thoughts; it was a boy.

'The boy's deteriorating,' said Mr Woodington.

'In what way, would you say?'

'Oh, in every way.'

Mr and Mrs Woodington were in their sitting-room at Hawthorn Hill with Mr Stokes, the Assistant Children's Officer. Mr Stokes was a large, blond, placid man from Suffolk who had taken up this appointment about six months previously, when Miss Horniman had her nervous breakdown. One of his duties was periodically to review the progress of all the children in the Homes and to assess whether they really needed to be there at all. He was in the armchair, with a scatter of files and Review Report forms in front of him.

'He's been here two years now and I'm blessed if I can see

what we're supposed to be doing for him,' said Mrs Woodington.

'H'm,' said Mr Stokes. 'Well, let's go through the headings on the form and see what emerges. No sign of the parents, I suppose?'

'No.'

'No other contacts?'

'No; we found an "aunt" for him, but he pilfered from her and she dropped him like a hot coal.'

'Attitude to parents?'

The Woodingtons considered. Mr Woodington said: 'Bitter.' Mrs Woodington said: 'Doesn't give a damn about them.' Mr Woodington added: 'Mind you, I sometimes suspect that deep down he'd like to find his mother; but I think his motive is to revenge himself upon her.'

Mr Stokes said: 'I don't think we could find her after all this time. Sounds as if it would be dangerous anyway. Relationship with staff?'

'There isn't one. Not a real relationship. He knows who's boss, mind: right at the beginning I had to put my foot down with a firm hand, and he's got some sort of grudging respect for me now.'

Mrs Woodington said: 'That's putting it mildly. He hates your guts, Fred.'

'Relationship with other children?'

'None.'

'Nasty. Cruel,' said Mr Woodington. 'He's at the bottom of all the trouble in this house and yet he can never be caught at it. He seems to love seeing the little ones get into hot water because of something he's made them do – he seems to love that.'

'Endearing child,' said Mr Stokes placidly. 'State of health?'

'Far too good,' said Mrs Woodington gloomily.

'Has puberty begun?'

'It began in his cradle, I should think,' sniffed the Superintendent. 'We really have to watch him with the girls, and the trouble is they all think he's the cat's pyjamas – I don't know why.'

'Interests and hobbies?'

'Girls. Smoking. Blackmail. Knives. Nothing sort of nice, you know; anything nice makes him look as though he wants to vomit.'

'Crumbs!' said Mr Stokes, rubbing his nose. 'A right beauty, isn't he? And he's due to leave here at the end of this term: what the devil are we going to do with him?'

'Drown him,' said Mrs Woodington, lighting another cigarette.

'Oh no, now let's be fair,' said her husband. 'There might be a chance for him during his teens. You know how with these kids sometimes everything clicks when they start out to work – he might suddenly choose the right road.'

'Yes; and pigs might fly.'

'And another thing, he's never been in trouble with the police; lord knows how, but he hasn't, and I feel that shows some sort of sense of right and wrong.'

'No, Fred,' said Mrs Woodington. 'He's a born crook and he'll be in trouble before he's through, I'm convinced of it.'

'What do you recommend for him?' asked Mr Stokes. 'I suppose a working boys' hostel would be the safest?'

'Well, I don't know what you think, Mr Stokes, but I feel that if he went to a hostel he'd gravitate at once to the worst kids there. Then he wouldn't stand a chance. If there is some chance of saving him, I reckon it might be done in a foster-home.'

'Oh; who'd take him? Be reasonable, Fred!'

'An experienced foster-mother, I mean; one of those who does it for money. Not one of these young flibbertigibbets – that wouldn't do. Anyway, I think the lad ought to be given the chance, and if he can't take it, well then at least he can't turn round and say we never let him try.'

Mr Stokes nodded. 'Yes, I think there's a lot in what you say, Mr Woodington. There are some old battle-scarred foster-mothers about who might give him a try. I'll put it round to the areas, and see what they can suggest, and then I'll come and see you again.'

He put the file thoughtfully to one side. 'Anyway,' he said,

'I doubt if we've heard the last of Archibald Tod. Now, then, who's next. Royston Carter Beedman.'

The Woodingtons immediately looked happier and stirred around to more comfortable positions. This was evidently a horse of a different colour.

'Now, this is another one with no parents, isn't it?' said Mr Stokes. 'No contact, I presume? No. Now – oh, this one's adopted, isn't he – does he know about that?'

Mr Woodington nodded. 'Yes, I told him all about it about a year ago. He took it surprisingly well, I thought; we haven't had any reaction at all really, have we, love?'

'Well – no.'

'What's he feel about the Beedman people?'

'It's rather hard to say,' said Mrs Woodington, slowly. 'The way I see Royston is, frankly, he's just staying here, he's not living here, he's sort of biding his time; but what he's biding his time for, I can't imagine. It might be that he thinks he's going home some day; what do you think, Fred?'

'I think he's written them off,' said the Superintendent decidedly. 'Never mentions 'em, never worries about being here, or not getting letters, not bitter or anything – I think he's just decided to go his own way, blow 'em.'

'What's his relationship with the staff?'

'Rather off-hand,' said Mrs Woodington. 'That's what I mean, he's not whole-heartedly belonging here. He's friendly – get him on his own, and you can have a real nice conversation with him. You did the other night, didn't you, Fred?'

'Ah – about the colour bar. It was a really pleasant adult conversation. Yet I know what the wife means. He's friendly and pleasant and yet somehow he's not sort of, well, *engaged*, if you see what I mean.'

'Ye-es.' Mr Stokes tapped thoughtfully with his ball-point pen. 'What about with other children?'

'Much the same. Quite well-liked, mixes, quite easily, very nice with the little ones, quarrels sometimes but nothing out the ordinary; and yet he's never had a real companion since he's been here, has he?'

'Well, except for Tod sometimes.'

'Tod?' asked Mr Stokes wonderingly. 'Don't tell me he's friendly with Tod? I should have thought they were as different as chalk from cheese.'

'Well, so they are on the whole, but every now and then Royston seems to want to be dragged down – oh, I don't know how to put this. What do you say, Doll?'

Mrs Woodington considered. Then she said: 'I s'pose this is going to sound a bit fanciful, but, you know, Tod in a way belongs to the dark side of life – anything decent and fair Tod will sort of reject and spit on. Now Royston, on the whole, belongs to the bright side, but every now and then he seems to want to go dark, and then he and Tod'll be as thick as thieves for a fortnight. Royston'll put on a rough, uncouth accent and leer at the girls and mooch about here – you've noticed, Fred, haven't you?'

'Ah. Funny really. Normally Royston's a very well-mannered lad – he'd been nicely brought up, I will say that – and then suddenly he has one of these spasms.'

'Odd,' said Mr Stokes, shaking his head. 'What next? Progress at school?'

'B stream. Plugs along. No complaints. Not much you can say under that head.'

'Health?'

'Keeps very well. He's growing very fast, by the way; he's going to be a big lad, I think.'

'Interests and hobbies?'

'Normal for his age, I'd say – football; aircraft spotting; collects matchbox labels; the cinema – he's mad keen on Marilyn Monroe, by the way. Sometimes he'll chase about playing cowboys, if he gets the wind in his tail, you know.'

'Interested in girls?'

'Not really, unless he's in one of his dark moods.'

Mr Stokes peered with a thoughtful frown at the notes he had made. 'This kid doesn't quite click with me,' he said. 'I can't quite see him somehow. He's plugging along satisfactorily in a way, and yet we don't seem to be solving anything really. Are you worried about this Tod business, this dark side stuff?'

'No, not really, it'll sort itself out when Tod leaves. Royston's basically a nice lad, I'm sure of that; it's just that he's sort of keeping himself for somebody.'

'Do you think he needs a foster-home?'

The Woodingtons considered this in silence.

'If you could take plenty of time over the introduction, plenty of week-ends and holidays, I would think yes,' said Mr Woodington. 'But I think that this is a boy you just can't rush into anything.'

'I have the feeling that he's not ready for fostering yet,' said the Matron. 'There's something in the past that he hasn't really sorted out.'

'Could it be his natural mother?' asked Mr Stokes.

'I dunno, I haven't a clue. This is really only feminine intuition, but somehow I feel that he's not ready to attach himself anywhere.'

'Perhaps he needs to go through some sort of purifying experience first.'

They were all silent for a while, meditating.

'The thing that strikes me,' said Mr Stokes, rifling through the file, 'is the lack of information about the adoptive parents; nobody's ever bothered to go and check up on what they're doing. I wonder if there's anything there?'

'I shouldn't think so,' said Mr Woodington. 'When she brought the boy in, Miss Strachan said the mother was absolutely poisonous.'

'The Probation Officer seems to think it's the father who's poisonous. I wonder. They had him for twelve years, after all.'

'I should lay off,' said the Superintendent. 'Let's have a clean break.'

'You can't have a clean break after twelve years.'

'Oh, I know, that's your modern theory – always come to terms with the past; but I think there's times when you must have a clean break and I think this is one of them. The boy's written 'em off; why don't you do the same?'

But Mr Stokes had made up his mind. 'Before we try any fostering I'd like to satisfy myself about those Beedmans. We've got to view the whole situation; the boy doesn't exist in a vacuum.'

'Oh well, please yourself. They live in Francombe New Town; do you know it?'

'No.'

'Well, there's the Old Town, which is just the original village on the main road; and then after the fourteen-eighteen war they built a sort of suburb for stockbrokers and nobs like that.'

'Good gracious, I thought you meant a real New Town, you know, like Stevenage.'

'Oh, no. This is quite nobby; you'll have to wear your best bib and tucker up there.'

'H'm. Not like my usual hunting-grounds. Right, then. I'll go and do a sort of recce up there and see what I get.'

'You'll be careful, won't you?'

'Oh, yes. I may get nowhere, of course. But I can't see that I shall do any harm.'

IO

MR STOKES did not immediately contact the Beedmans. For one thing he had a large number of cases to deal with, and this particular job did not seem of desperate urgency; for another, he was fairly sure that when he did go to see them he would get rebuffed, and there were several days when he might have gone but just felt that he could not possibly stand anyone else spitting at him. But in the end he went to the office one morning bracing himself, telling himself that this had to be got over; and so he rang up Mrs Beedman.

He had decided, after browsing through the file and noticing particularly Dr Maclaren's remarks at the case conference, that she was the one to go for, and that if possible he would tackle her while her husband was at work. When she answered the telephone, he put on his most astringent Oxford accent and asked for an appointment.

'What's it about?'

'I'm representing the County Council,' purred Stokes. 'I wonder if you could possibly spare me an hour one morning?'

'My husband won't be here, you know.'

'No, quite; it was you I wanted to see, Mrs Beedman.'

'Look, what is this? Who are you?'

'I am the Assistant Children's Officer,' announced Stokes, grandly.

'You mean it's about *Royston*,' she said, with great bitterness.

'It was more about yourself,' said Stokes, letting a slightly lecherous note creep into his voice.

After a fidgety silence she agreed, petulantly, to see him the following morning. She sounded intrigued, but by no means enthusiastic.

Mr Stokes dressed himself carefully in his best blue suit and sauntered up to the door of Twelvetrees exactly one minute before the time appointed.

She wouldn't let him in at first. 'Is this trouble?' she snapped at the door.

'Trouble, ma'am?' he asked, leaning forward deferentially.

'You know what I mean, don't act. Is that boy on the loose again?'

'Royston? Oh no. Oh no, nothing like that.'

She let him in, still very suspicious, and led the way into the lounge. She'd got herself up for him, he realized, in her beige suit and alligator shoes. She was a thin, tall woman with carefully tinted fair hair and a bright artificial complexion. Her mouth was sulky.

'Look, come clean, will you? What is all this? It *is* about Royston, isn't it? What's all the mystery?'

'It is about Royston, in a way,' he admitted, as elegantly as he could. 'You see, when I came to check up on my colleagues I realized that none of them had really tried to study your feelings in this matter, to hear your angle on the boy.'

'So what? What's my angle got to do with it?'

'Well, you see,' he drawled, 'as you know, we have got to plan for this boy in the future and it seemed to me that you had the right to be consulted about that.'

'Are you trying to swing him back on to me, is that it? Because I'm not having him.'

'Oh, good lord, no, Mrs Beedman, one quite realizes that. No, to be absolutely frank with you,' he said, cursing himself for his hypocrisy, 'you must have seen him at his worst, and therefore you could probably advise us what to look out for in the future.'

She gazed at him narrowly: she couldn't quite make him out. Up till then she had thought of a social worker as approximately on a par with a gas-man or a plumber. This chap seemed to be fairly high up in the world, rather well-bred; and yet nothing he said rang quite true – there was something phoney somewhere.

'You'd better sit down,' she said at length, taking the chair by the window and crossing her legs.

There was a pause.

'Of course, you know Royston isn't mine?' she said.

'Well, I knew he was adopted,' he replied cautiously.

'Yes. He was adopted. We gave him that chance and it didn't work out; we don't feel any responsibility now, you know.'

'Quite so.' He produced the cigarette case with which he had equipped himself that morning – he had actually given up smoking about a year before. He lit her cigarette for her and she gave him an automatic upward glance; an almost imperceptible trace of intimacy had crept in.

'Thank you,' she said.

There was another pause. He was waiting like a cat at a mousehole.

'What's bred in the bone comes out in the whatever it is,' she said. 'That's what we didn't realize.'

'Forgive my asking, Mrs Beedman, but did the boy come from an Adoption Society?'

She shook her head, taking a long pull on her cigarette. 'No. We were living in Norwood at the time. Gilbert was on warwork – he'd just got a big contract for supplying uniforms, and I hardly ever saw him. And there was this girl. I only met her once; my daily woman told me about her. Apparently she was trying to get an abortion done. Oh, I was a fool.'

Mr Stokes was not enjoying his cigarette, but he made one or two brave, relaxed puffs at it. He was keeping very quiet.

'You wouldn't understand, I suppose. But there was that damned great house, and Gilbert always away somewhere. I must have been mad.'

'You couldn't have children?' he asked very quietly. It was a crucial question: if she took offence now he'd had it.

'I had a miss,' she said.

She suddenly leant forward and crushed out her half-smoked cigarette with an air almost of defiance. 'I had a miss at five months, a bad one, it nearly killed me,' she said. 'So –' She shrugged and gave a deep sigh.

The glance he gave her had in it the first gleam of genuine sympathy. 'How did your husband feel about the adoption?' he asked quietly.

She shot him a hard angry glance, and he thought he'd lost her.

'Look,' she said. 'Gilbert's a good husband; a good provider; anything I want he'll get for me in the end, if he can. Look at this place. With me behind him he's come a long way. He's got nothing to be ashamed of.'

'No, indeed. You have a very charming home.'

'But he didn't like the idea. Never did take to it.'

She was silent for a moment, looking at the tip of her shoe. 'Are you married?'

'Yes,' said Mr Stokes comfortably.

'Any children?'

'Two. Two boys.'

The mixed expressions which captured her face – pleasure, disgust, pain, envy – said, as loudly as if she had spoken, 'That's more than Gilbert can do.' She gave him an eerie glance which flickered all over-his body. Then she stood up impatiently and said : 'Will you have some coffee?'

'Thank you!' said Stokes, in a pleased voice.

While she was getting it, he pondered what he had heard. He had noticed that when she was revealing something her accent slipped down a couple of pegs; for that last remark it had definitely gone back up. He was afraid the interview might be nearly over.

She came back with the coffee and he gave her another cigarette and had one himself, though his head was still swimming from the first one. She sipped away quietly and seemed to be waiting for him to say something. He chose a neutral subject : 'What a very charming room!'

'You like it?' she said indifferently. 'It's not bad, I suppose; I shall probably change it all round soon. Every now and then I get in a mood and change everything round.'

'You have sudden impulses like that?'

'A bar in that corner, I thought, quite amusing. I know what I want.'

'You're an impulsive person, would you say?'

'Or I might move, get the hell out of here.'

'Really? It seems, to an outsider, quite a pleasant place.'

'We-ell, I suppose so. I feel fed up sometimes. I know one thing, I'm not stopping here till the day I die.'

'No, I see. Are your family living in this neighbourhood?'

'Let's leave my family out of this, do you mind?' She took a hard-beaked peck at her coffee. 'What did you want to know about Royston?'

Mr Stokes heaved a small sigh and asked: 'His real name?'

'Butcher, Baker, something like that.'

'It was his mother's name?'

'It was what she called herself. I believe she'd taken the man's name.'

'And she was a young girl, you said?'

'Seventeen.'

'And how old was the baby when he was handed over?'

'Ten days.'

'Did the mother bring the baby?'

'No, Matron came from the Nursing Home.'

'Oh, Royston was born in a Nursing Home?'

'Yes. We paid.'

'I see.' Mr Stokes had now realized that she was happier giving short answers to direct questions – evidently his first cat-and-mouse act had unsettled her. He wasn't quite sure what he was driving at himself, but he pushed on. 'Did the mother ever know where the baby had gone?'

'What do you think we are? We didn't want her hanging around, thank you very much.'

'And in fact, she never did bother you?'

'Of course not.'

'The adoption went through smoothly?'

'Of course.'

'At Norwood?'

'Look here, you're not going to try and find that blasted mother now, are you? I may not be responsible for the boy, but there are some things I will not allow!'

'No, no, Mrs Beedman, of course not, please don't answer anything which embarrasses you; it is very good of you to help me.'

'We had it done at Chipham, as a matter of fact,' she said in a sober voice. 'I knew the old boy there and slipped him a fiver to get it through quick for us, which he did.'

'Quite so. Now : after Royston had come to you, all went well at first?'

'Oh, it never – well – I suppose in a way – oh, say yes, then.' This confused sentence had evidently cost her something: she had had reluctantly to make an admission. She stubbed out her cigarette, fished out one of her own filter-tips and lit it, not offering him one, though in any case he didn't want it. She puffed rapidly and went on : 'Yes, it was all right at first. Gilbert never took to him, I told you that; I know why too, but that's no business of yours.'

'Did the baby cry much, or cause any difficulty? Was his development normal, I mean?'

'I suppose it was.' She studied the burning tip of her cigarette. 'You see, in those days I had someone – well, actually my sister, living with us. She helped me with the baby; if Gil wanted to go out in the evening, it was O.K., I could go too. It was when we moved the trouble started.'

'You came out here then?'

'No; we went to Hampstead, just after the war. It was a flat, and there wasn't room for my sister. That was a good thing in one way. We were paying the earth for that place, but we could manage it; Gil had got a new partnership, and he was going ahead fast. It was one of those no dogs, no children, no radiogram places. Hell!'

She was puffing away with the cigarette wagging between her lips, and sweeping flecks of ash from her smooth tight skirt.

'We'd have been all right if the bloody kid had cooperated. That was all I asked. Whine, whine, whine all day. It drove me up the wall! We had to move. Gil was furious – well, so was I, another twelve months and we'd have cleaned up a packet on the f. and f.'

'You came to Francombe?'

'No! Thornton Heath. It was all we could get. Look, this may sound selfish to you; maybe it sounds all wrong to someone in your position, but I don't care: Gil was losing money over that place, he couldn't take his business contacts home to that dump.

He was losing hundreds and I stood to lose everything I'd fought for. It was my husband or the child and say what you like I stood by that child – my conscience is clear.'

'I'm quite sure you did all you could, Mrs Beedman.'

'Of course I did. Went down on my knees to the neighbours, literally on my knees to get a baby-sitter for him! And a foster-mother! I paid a foster-mother, me, in my position, a foster-mother! Nobody can say I didn't do everything in my power.'

She stubbed out her cigarette crossly, but went on more calmly, reflectively picking shreds of tobacco off her tongue: 'Well, then we got the place in Dulwich and I fixed him up with a nursery school, and then of course he got old enough to be left in the evenings. Gil got back on his feet again. He was good to that kid, you know. After all, there was no reason why he should have been when it was another man's child, which Gil could never swallow; but anyway he was good to him. Money going whenever he could spare it into an education endowment policy, for fees, you know – he wanted the best for the boy even if he wasn't his own. He wanted to get for that boy what he'd never had himself – proper education; he slaved for that. And what did dear little Royston do?'

She leaned forward and glared at him. Her jaws seemed to be clenched. 'Defiance, I've never seen such defiance! What had he got to be defiant about? He would stand there and lie to me; and the lies he told! I'm telling you, something I've never told another living soul. The things I've had to put up with from that boy! Nobody else in this world would have stood it from a child, least of all from one who was not her own. He'd steal from my bag and then stand there and face me out, swear black was white he'd never had the money! Gil doesn't know half of what I put up with, not a quarter. I dared not tell him – he'd have killed that boy. I did all in my power to break him – you've got to with children. In the end it got to the pitch where he had to choose – either he broke or he went his own sweet way. Well, you know what he chose. I warned him, time and again I warned him, but it was water off a duck's back. O.K., then, it was up to him after that, I couldn't care less. My conscience was clear.'

After this dam-burst of narrative, Stokes was somewhat at a loss as to how to proceed. He sat nodding and grunting quietly for a bit without looking at her, to give her a chance to get over her trembling, and then decided to use a trusty old gambit. Rising to his feet, he said: 'Well, I'm afraid I've taken up a terrible amount of your time, Mrs Beedman, I'm so sorry.'

'That's all right.'

'I'm afraid I do talk an awful lot.'

'Oh, well: you've got your job to do.'

She had grown shy of him; her walk to the door to show him out was hesitant. He said, reassuringly: 'You know, strictly between you and me, Mrs Beedman, but some of these children aren't really up to it. You can't make a silk purse out of a sow's ear.'

'I suppose that's true.'

'A pity, of course; he'd have had every advantage if he'd been able to make the grade.'

She shrugged.

'Still, I'm sure you've got a lot to be thankful for,' he said. 'House, car, good company.'

'M'm.'

'I suppose it's just that sometimes it feels as though something's missing?'

She gave a hard, suspicious look all round her domain. 'What is?' she asked.

Mr Stokes gave a deep sigh and took his leave of her.

II

MISS MOLE began by writing to the Reception Home at Banns Cross, for this was the only address she had. After ten days she had a letter back from the Shire Hall saying that Royston was in the care of the County Council and was no longer at Banns Cross; all communications should be addressed impersonally to the Children's Officer, quoting P. This was signed by the Administrative Officer in a violent scrawl she could not decipher.

She wrote back – impersonally, quoting P – asking if she could become a foster-mother and explaining that she went to work in the mornings only but didn't have to. She immediately got a postcard back, telling her that her communication was to hand and was receiving attention, date as postmark.

After another ten days she had a letter thanking her for her communication undated, and pointing out that prospective foster-parents were required to furnish full particulars of their circumstances together with a medical testimonial and the names of three referees. She gathered that her letter had been forwarded to the appropriate Divisional Officer, from whom doubtless she would hear further in due course. The letter concluded by pointing out that it was not the policy of the County Council to encourage applications from those not engaged in full-time household duties. This was also signed by the illegible Administrative Officer.

A fortnight after this, at nine o'clock at night, Miss Mole was watching a programme on television appealing for foster-homes when there was a loud knock on the door and in came a wild-eyed woman who said she was a Child Care Officer and could Miss Mole take in, there and then, a fifteen-year-old girl who was pregnant? Miss Mole was in a quandary. She had not the slightest compassion for trewsed and gum-chewing girls; on the other hand, she assumed that this might be some sort of initiation test for foster-parents devised by the County Council which already ran the 11-plus. So she agreed. The girl ran away on the second day, taking with her a pound note from under the clock; Miss Mole was not sure if she had passed her test or not.

Two weeks later she got from Shire Hall, a large cheque for 14s. 3d. with a printed slip saying: *Fuchsia La Froy: 2/7 weeks' maintenance @ 50s.* Miss Mole crumpled this up and hurled it across the room. Later, thinking better of it, she retrieved it and smoothed it out, deciding wryly that she would frame it and hang it in the spare bedroom. Later still, being thrifty, she cashed it.

When another three weeks had drifted by without any communication whatever, Miss Mole got on the bus and went over to Perkhampton.

The Shire Hall was a low, sprawling conglomeration of asbestos huts, hurriedly run up around the remains of the original building, which had been bombed. The imposing door in the centre, which Miss Mole tried first, was locked. Farther to the north she found another one which did open, on to a long corridor; she walked down this without seeing a soul and emerged at the other end into the open air again.

Turning up her coat collar against the gale, Miss Mole blew down to the south-west corner, where, half-way along the side of another hut, she saw a door banging regularly in the wind. On going in, she found herself among a throng of girls and youths who were walking about carrying tea-trays. She inquired for the Children's Department; the first person she asked had never heard of it, but the second, a keen youth with huge spectacles, said it was in the Finance Department and if she went left, then left again and up the stairs, she would find a porter who would direct her. She followed the instructions, but no porter was visible, so she hunted about and eventually found the Finance Department all by herself. But they said they were sorry, it wasn't there, and if she would go to the East Door there was a porter there who would show her the way. Twenty minutes later, Miss Mole descended into a basement, actually the cellars of the old building, and so at last was ushered into a little corner office, with an iron grille in the roof, over which incessantly clanged the feet of pedestrians in the street above.

A large, blond, tired man greeted her with a smile.

'Hallo,' he said. 'Do sit down. I say, I'm just going to have a cup of tea, will you have some?'

Miss Mole sank thankfully on to the chair. 'Thank you very much,' she said, 'I'm sure.'

Mr Stokes secured an extra cup of tea and got her settled and offered her a cigarette, for he was now smoking quite heavily again, and asked how he could help her.

'Well,' she said, 'it's about a boy called Royston.'

'Oh, yes: Charlie Royston or Royston Beedman?'

'Royston Beedman,' she said, her face lighting up. 'Do you know him? How is he?'

'I don't know the boy very well, I'm afraid. I know the case. How did you come to hear about him?'

'Well, it was rather a strange thing, you see. I don't know, I hope you'll tell me if I'm poking my nose in where I oughtn't to, only I feel sorry for that boy.'

'Where did you meet him?'

'It was before he came into your hands,' said Miss Mole. 'I don't know if you remember, but he did a silly thing in East Whixham – he broke into a house.'

'Oh, yes, I remember; he was on the loose at the time, wasn't he? He'd run away from home.'

'That's right. Well, he broke in and, well, it was me that called the police. I felt terrible afterwards when I saw the poor little mite, only you see I had a room in Priory Gardens at the time and I looked out and I saw this window open at Mr Patton's and matches lighting, y'see, well, I knew they were away. So I called Mr Chance, that was the landlord where I lived, and we telephoned the police and then we both went round. Well, I mean wouldn't you, all this crime about, I mean you can't not, can you?'

'No,' said Mr Stokes, disentangling this. 'But I can't see why you should reproach yourself, Miss Mole. After all, the boy was doing very wrong and he had to be stopped.'

'Oh, yes, but – well, I mean, I went round fully expecting to see some great rough man in a striped jersey, and there all it was was this poor litle creature crouching on the stairs with his little peaky face, frightened half out of his wits. I can see him now, and I thought, well, I thought, I shouldn't have done it.'

Mr Stokes did not answer but leaned his chin on his hand and scowled thoughtfully at her. He couldn't make out what this was leading up to.

'And then, in the Court!' she went on, 'Mr Chance and me had to go in case we were needed as witnesses, and when I saw that woman – when I saw that woman, Mr Stokes, calling herself his mother – well, then I saw what the matter was, and how he only wanted loving-kindness, and I cried.'

'I think he needed more than loving-kindness,' murmured Mr Stokes. 'Then what?'

'I knew he was going to Banns Cross, so I rang up there and Mr Lloyd was really rather sharp; well, I can't blame him either, after all I *was* poking my nose in and I couldn't anyway have been much help, I couldn't have been a foster-mother, not in one room like that. So I had to let it go. But then the extraordinary thing is, Mr Stokes, that I've been fortunate enough to inherit some money, enough for what I need, and now I've got my own little bungalow, so I reely could help after all, if I was allowed to, I mean.'

'I see,' said Mr Stokes. 'You're interested in becoming a foster-mother?'

'Yes, I am. I'd like to try and help a child – mind you, I don't reely want any more like that Fuchsia –' and Miss Mole told about her adventures so far; 'but if I could I'd like to have Royston. There was a sort of special link between us – I mean even when first I saw him my heart sort of turned over. It was – well, it was almost as if he was my son.'

Miss Mole was pink with embarrassment.

Mr Stokes gazed at her thoughtfully. He was interested in this case; he liked the honest apple cheeks of Miss Mole; he felt bad about the off-hand treatment she had so far received; he remembered very clearly that Royston had nothing to look forward to in his own house – yet he was pretty sure that Royston needed a man, a father-figure; and he remembered that many sentimental spinsters try to take up a foster-child as they might a stray cat; and he reflected that guilt is not the best basis to build a foster home on. These thoughts went through his mind like an express train, each thought banging like a carriage.

'Well, first I must thank you very much for coming forward, Miss Mole,' he said at last, gravely. 'You'll appreciate that this has rather taken me by surprise; I shall have to think about it.'

'Oh, yes, I wouldn't want to rush into anything. How is the boy, Mr Stokes?'

'He's all right, you know. No more trouble; he's settled down in the Home. Of course, he's only got a few more months to go now before he has to leave school and start out somewhere on his own. He can't return home.'

'Ooh, I'm sure. That never was a home, not like I understand home.'

'Quite. You had a happy home yourself, Miss Mole?'

'Yes, Mr Stokes, I did. I was very fortunate, I realize. Mind you, we were poor at times; sometimes Dad did very well, but sometimes we were very hard up indeed. Only the thing was, when I look back, we were always so cheery – me and Horry and Mum and Dad, we always seemed to fit in together comfortably, even when food was so short during the War, before rationing started – you wouldn't remember those times, but they was pretty grim; and yet you know we stayed cheery. I always had the dream, even when I was quite a little girl, that one day I'd set up a home just like that. Sounds silly, I suppose.'

'You never married, Miss Mole?'

'No; things never quite worked out,' she said. 'Horry went abroad, you see, and after Dad died I stayed looking after Mum, and so I never in the end got around to getting wed. I often wish – oh well, there it is. Mind you, I've had my moments; I wouldn't call myself an old maid.'

'I'm sure not, Miss Mole,' chuckled Stokes. 'Well now, first of all, Mr Ponto was quite right to point out to you that we have to have these references and medical reports. I'm sorry if it sounds like red tape, but it is the law and I can't move at all till it's done.'

'Quite so, sir.'

'The next thing, assuming the inquiries we shall make into your circumstances are satisfactory, is that I shall have to consider whether another child might not fit in better with you than Royston. I realize that you've got a special interest in Royston, but there may be another child whom you could help more than him.'

'I don't think there could be, Mr Stokes, but you know best.'

'You must appreciate, Miss Mole, that this Royston Beedman is not *now* the frightened little boy you remember; he's a young chap now. And young chaps, you know, need fathers.'

'Yes, I do see that, sir. I am at a great disadvantage there; but then if a lad's never had a mother, surely he might –?'

'Oh, yes, Miss Mole, I'm not saying this is impossible, but there is one final thing you have to face, and that is that although you have a very special affection for this boy, he may not feel the same about you – in fact, he may feel just the opposite. And that could hurt, Miss Mole.'

She gave a deep sigh. 'Oh lord, Mr Stokes, you make it sound very hard, and I'm sure what you say is sensible. And yet you know I feel deep down that I could give Royston something he hasn't ever known and that he would, well, take to it.'

'Very well, Miss Mole,' said Mr Stokes, making up his mind as the train of objections in his brain sang past and way on down the line, 'here's what we'll do: I'll fill in the Foster-parents' Circumstances Form and take up the references. If all's well, I'll arrange for Royston to come and stay with you for weekends, one weekend in three –'

'Couldn't he come every one? I'd willingly –'

'I have to think of the other children in the Home who never go out anywhere, Miss Mole; let's be fair. One in three; then you'll have the chance to get to know him well – after all you've not even spoken to him yet. And for his part he'll have a break and a bit of individual attention and I expect a bit of fuss made of him too, and that won't do any harm.'

'I like the idea very much, Mr Stokes; I'll certainly play my part.'

'Good. I'm making two conditions, Miss Mole: if the boy tells me he doesn't want to come, I shan't let him come, and if by any chance I find a married couple who want a boy of this age and who would suit Royston, I shall give them priority. If you would regard yourself as the boy's godmother, Miss Mole, how does that strike you?'

'Godmother, sir, yes, that's just what I would like to be, thank you.'

And Miss Mole duly took her leave and plunged out into a howling gale, the air full of yellow leaves, feeling very much happier than when she went in. In due course her references came back saying that she was sober, industrious, warm-hearted and free from T.B., and Mr Stokes arranged the first weekend. He decided to drive the boy down himself in his car, and the reflection crossed his mind that he was taking rather a risk, relying on his own judgement that Miss Mole was not the sort of person to set out to bribe the boy, with money and emotion, never, never to leave her for a mere married couple.

They arrived in time for lunch on the Saturday, a meal being a good way to break the ice, and Mr Stokes stayed too. Royston ate quickly and deftly, busy with his own thoughts, answering politely but shortly if he was spoken to. Afterwards, when Mr Stokes had departed, having helped with the washing up, Miss Mole said: 'Now, Royston, what I like doing on a Saturday afternoon is stroll down to the front and sit down quietly and watch the people. So you come on too and we'll see what we shall see, and at five o'clock we'll have an egg and chips at Bunty's.'

So they strolled down together. Royston made no attempt to strike up a conversation, and Miss Mole, who believed in letting things go at their own pace, did not intrude upon him. She settled herself in a deck chair and he went off to the boating lake and skimmed up and down in a kayak. After that he went on the crazy golf and after that he threw stones in the sea. He had what he would need to the end of his life: a period of solitude with a time-limit to it, so that control and blessed order were not far away.

Presently he came nosing up to Miss Mole's deck chair and said: 'Is this a flint arrow-head?'

'It looks very much like it,' said Miss Mole. 'You've got very sharp eyes, I'd never have spotted that. Only what I can't understand is, how did an arrow-head come to be on a beach?'

Royston reflected. 'Perhaps a hunter chased a stag down here and it flew into the sea. They do do that when they're frightened. Nowadays, they bring tommy-guns and finish 'em off.'

'So I've heard,' said Miss Mole comfortably. 'Doesn't seem fair on the stag.'

'No, it doesn't, does it?' said Royston after a pause.

He went off to look for crabs under the breakwater.

At five o'clock they went and got their egg and chips and Miss Mole said diffidently that she had thought of going to the pictures in the evening, how did Royston feel about coming? When he heard it was a Burt Lancaster picture, Royston became very enthusiastic; he had gone off Marilyn Monroe. Miss Mole said they would be rather late coming out: he had better have another egg and chips now. Roystons' eyes glistened.

He had never in his life before been taken to the pictures alone by an adult. He had never before stayed right to the end, when they play the National Anthem. He had never before trotted home legitimately through the dark and windy streets when lots of grown-up people were already in bed. There was a certain air of conspiracy about it all.

Miss Mole was careful to get up first in the morning and brought him a cup of tea in bed. Royston was both pleased and embarrassed. After breakfast she asked what he felt about church. Royston looked at her calculatingly: he didn't know what would please her. So he said tentatively: 'At the Home we go every Sunday.'

'Well, you're not in the Home this weekend, so I expect you'd like to do a bit different for a change. Mind you, I like going; we'll both go some time, when we're in the mood.'

Royston was relieved. Sometimes people you like sing most embarrassingly loud in church. He fetched a bucket of coke for her.

They walked down together to the newsagent's to fetch the paper and spent half an hour before lunch tut-tutting over the cases. After lunch they listened to 'Educating Archie', and then there was a lot of garden rubbish and bits of stuff the builders had left to be gathered together and burnt. Royston enjoyed fire-raising and to keep the bonfire going he collected stuff from all over the neighbourhood. He was sorry when it was time to clean up and walk down to the station. He became constrained and quiet and settled down in the carriage with his nose in a comic. When the train started he looked up for a moment and waved perfunctorily. Miss Mole's heart turned over; but she believed in letting things go at their own pace.

It was surprising how quickly the weekends came round. Miss Mole was not obsessed with Royston; she only wrote to him when she had something to say, and he never wrote back, but every third weekend she found herself meeting the train with pleasurable anticipation, and out of the train he would come, smiling shyly. Some things they did every week-end traditionally, like the egg and chips at Bunty's, but she always tried to arrange one thing different each time. Once she got a ticket to a Jazz Concert for him: he went by himself and she waited up for him. Once he came obsessed with Monopoly and would do nothing else but play it all the time, cheating like mad. Once she took him to a dance, but that was a mistake – he was miserable with shyness. Once he cancelled the weekend altogether because he wanted to go with the other children to a Works Christmas party. Once he came in a deep, dark, sullen mood and she was nearly reduced to tears.

It was an unsatisfying period for Miss Mole. He came, they chatted, they got on comfortably, and he went; and every time she felt that she had made no progress whatever. There was a deep, large, unengaged part of this boy that she never got near. Sometimes he would mention incidents that had occurred at the Home, or in school; sometimes he would see a place on the television and would mention that he had once been there, or passed through it. Once, when there was a play on the radio all about a girl with no parents, a horrible curtain of embarrassment fell between them. Often there were long periods when Royston answered her conversation and yet seemed to be listening to other voices in his own head. Miss Mole would come sadly back from seeing him off on the train and wonder if she ought to put an end to the whole thing; she was doing no good.

At Easter Mr Stokes blew in for a chat. She told him faithfully all that had been happening. 'You're doing a wonderful job, Miss Mole, believe me.'

'You surprise me, Mr Stokes, you reelly do. I was thinking of packing it up.'

'For goodness' sake don't do that, Miss Mole! You mean a great deal to Royston, though you mayn't realize it.'

'Does he talk much about me, at the Home?'

'Well, no, not much; but he comes toddling off to you every third week-end; it takes a lot to make him put that off. You're his anchor at the moment, Miss Mole, and he'll drift on to the rocks if you let go.'

'I don't seem to be getting anywhere near him, though.' She described how she felt about his remoteness.

'That'll come right in the end, Miss Mole, don't you worry. After all, this kid's had a rough time. A burnt child fears the fire. He's been let down badly once, and he won't trust another human being in a hurry. But he's beginning to trust you; you're dependable. For goodness' sake, please don't let go now.'

'No, of course not, Mr Stokes, I'm very pleased to hear what you say, of course. But I think there's something else bothering Royston. I think he's got something on his mind.'

'Any sort of clue what it is, Miss Mole?'

'It's only a hunch, Mr Stokes, maybe it's crazy, I don't know. But I think he wants to get hold of his mother.'

'Good lord: the *Beedman* woman?'

'Ooh, no. His real mother. I think he wants to find her and know where he stands.'

'But he can't! That's all over and done with; anyway nobody will ever be able to trace her now!'

'All the same, Mr Stokes, that's what I think's the matter. He'll never let himself belong anywhere else till he knows he doesn't belong to her.'

And Miss Mole found herself unexpectedly blowing her nose.

12

'ROYSTON! Royston! Have you seen Royston, Doll?'

'No,' said Mrs Woodington absently. 'I expect he's over in the shrubbery. I wonder what he finds to do there so often?'

'Smoking,' said Mr Woodington shortly. 'Or playing about.'

'Oh, don't be filthy, Fred. What do you want with him, anyway?'

'Nothing, really; just to run down with the letters; Jimmy'll go, won't you, Jim?'

'Wossart, sir?'

'Take these letters down to the pillar-box, will you, Jim? Please? I was going to ask Royston, it's his turn.'

'O.K., sir. Sir, 'e's gorn out, sir.'

'Who has? Royston has? Now what the devil's all that in aid of; he hasn't asked permission.'

'Sir, I don't know, sir.'

'All right, Jim, you nip along; the post goes in five minutes.' Mr Woodington told his wife that Royston had apparently drifted off, and she said: 'He's not gone on the loose, has he?'

'Oh, no. He's over all that lark. I expect he's got a date with a girl up the lane somewhere.'

This was not so, however. Royston had a date with Tod.

There was, commanding the railway cutting, an old concrete gun-post, a pill-box of a place used by the whole neighbourhood, by young ones and dogs as a lavatory, by older ones as a rendezvous. On the roof of this Royston was waiting, lying on his stomach with a foot wagging in the air; his chin was cupped in one hand and he traced out the patterns of moss with his other forefinger. He was wearing his Sunday best clothes, grey flannel trousers with a knife-edge crease, discreet green sports jacket, black shoes, a green-and-crimson paisley tie. His hair was flattened down with oil and his parting gleamed whitely.

He was enjoying the peace and quiet of the afternoon, with only an occasional Sunday train sauntering along the cutting.

Royston had now been at Hawthorn Hill for two and a half years and he was almost fifteen. He often surprised himself with these facts: the years had gone by unnoticed. He had grown considerably taller and was often unable to gauge the length of his own arms and legs and would knock things over. His voice had broken. After an initial period of panic at the thought of growing-up, he experienced a fierce exultation, that he was finished with childhood, that soon he would be leaving school and leaving the Home. The idea filled him with something between pleasure and terror.

He had not really enjoyed his years at Hawthorn Hill, and yet these had been nothing to cause him distress either. He liked Mr and Mrs Woodington; they were kindly and very fair, and they were obviously in control of the Home – he always knew where he stood with them. They were also extremely dull, and he never felt that he wanted to become a man like Mr Woodington or to marry a woman like the Matron: the lives they led and the job they did simply had no relevance to his own future. Imperceptibly, almost, he had advanced within the Home to the position of Senior Boy. When he occasionally thought of this beforehand he anticipated that he would presently move much closer to the Woodingtons, be an adult along with them; when he reached the position, he slowly realized that there was nothing to move closer to. It was then that he began to work out how it was that he had advanced to seniority – by the steady erosion of boys older than himself, who, one by one, had set off, cheerful but quaking, into the Outside World, and by his own inexorable advance towards the same point of insecurity. The departure of Tod, his immediate senior and crony for some years, had brought all this home to him with a jolt. Almost at once, Mr Woodington had started having little chats with him; stuffing tobacco into his pipe, he would say thoughtfully: 'You're the next one, Royston.' One could almost hear the tumbrils rumbling. 'You must have a good think about your future, boy; how do you fancy working in a factory?' Royston's image of a factory was roughly that of the ninth Lord Shaftesbury: he shook his head decisively. 'Well, you think about it, lad, and let us know; after all, we can't help you unless you tell us how we can help you, you see what I mean?' No! thought Royston wildly, even while he nodded his head; how the devil can I tell you when I don't know what I want or who I am or where I belong? He went into a black mood – you don't understand, you don't understand. 'You'll have to snap out of this if you want to make good in the world, Beedman.'

Beedman! Beedman, Beedman, Beedman, morning, noon, and night, that bloody name! He was known everywhere by it, he was trapped by it; this lot here preserved the lie and went on using the name and yet it wasn't his; he'd never asked to be saddled with it, he didn't like it, he thought it had a niminy-piminy sound. And yet, take away Beedman and what was he? What *was* he?

His reverie was interrupted by the sound of a bike crashing into the wall of the gun-post and Tod came scrambling up beside him.

'Oi, Roy!'

'Lo, Tod.'

Royston regarded the older boy with pleasure. Tod was wearing tight black jeans, black and white canvas boots known as bumpers, and a black jersey with an elaborate design all over the breast and shoulders, once white, now dark grey.

' 'Ow's Belsen? 'Ow's the ole master of slavery?'

'All right.'

'I dunno 'ow you stick it, I dunno 'ow I stuck it anyway. Bet you'll be glad to be out of it.'

Royston shrugged. 'Dunno. How you making out, Tod?'

'Orright. Movin'.'

'You are? What for?'

'Got slung out me lodge.'

'Coo! Why?'

'Well, see, the ole girl conceived a 'opeless passion for me, and o' course she 'ad to think of 'er reputation in the neighbourhood, so course I 'ad to go.' Tod did not like to give the real reason for his eviction, which was that he wouldn't wash himself.

'Coo!' What a romantic figure this Tod was, thought Royston; like him or not, you had to admire him. 'Where you going now then, Tod?'

'Chipham.'

'Chipham!' Something like a red-hot wire exclamation-mark appeared in Royston's brain.

'Yeah. 'Nother bloody ole foster-home. Archer found it for me.' Mr Archer was the local Child Care Officer. 'S'all right reelly. I'm goin' there Friday, that's why I come to see yer.'

'Cor, thanks for letting me know, Tod.' Tod gave him a bright, pitying look; he hadn't come here for Royston's benefit.

'You're me mate, aincha, Roy?'

'Yes,' said Royston reluctantly.

'Wancha to do somfing for me.'

'What?' said Royston, all suspicion.

'Oh, don't bark at me, it's nothin'. Anybody'd do it for me; be glad to.'

'What?'

'Shan't tell yer now. I thought I could rely on you. Never mind, Jimmy'll do it for me. You'll be sorry.'

'Oh, for God's sake, Tod, what?'

'Nothin'. Oh, well, if you reelly must know. Listen, you go to B.B. Wednesdays, don't yer?'

'Yes.'

'Well, this Wednesday I wancha to stop behind after. 'Ide in the 'ut.'

'Whatever for? I'll get copped for being out late.'

'No, you won't. Anyway, it's worth it. Jus' stop be'ind there, that's all you gotta do. 'Ide in amongst the camp stuff.'

'But *why*?'

'Shan't tell yer till yer say yer'll do it.'

Royston screwed his face up in an agony of thought. Tod watched him covertly and at the psychological moment said: 'You'll earn a quid.'

'A *quid*?'

'Well, less my commission, o' course,' said Tod, cursing himself for having started the bidding too high.

Royston's mind was now racing, not in an attempt to see what

Tod was driving at, but in a review of the opportunities this suddenly afforded him.

'Well?'

'All right, Tod; but what's it all about?'

'You've said you'd do it, so you're in it now. You let me down, Roy, and I'll do you up. Now, listen –'

Tod broke off suddenly to stare at a big-bosomed girl on a bicycle who was pedalling over the railway bridge.

'Cor, take a look at those!' The girl's face was pink and sweaty and her hair bright orange; but Tod never looked at girls' faces.

'Oh, never mind that, Tod, tell me about this job.'

'Well then, you gotta stay behind after B.B.; that's easy; make out you're going to the toilet and then nip in under them ole tents. Pricey'll never see yer.' Mr Price was Captain of the local Boys' Brigade. 'Then, after ole Pricey's gorn, when you 'ear me 'oot like an owl, nip out and open the 'ut door for me, that's all you gotta do; I'll give yer the ten bob and then you can scarper.'

'You said a quid.'

'I said less my commission.'

'A quid; or I'll split on you.'

'You wouldn't dare. Oh, all right, a quid, you miserable sod.' Tod was being paid five pounds for his part in arranging all this, and was prepared to give way when cornered.

Royston looked at him sidelong. He had found out how to get information from Tod. 'I bet it's just kids' stuff, anyway.'

'It is not bloody kids' stuff, mate! This is the big time. I'm in with a big mob, I am!'

'Get away!'

'You stick around Wednesday night an' you'll see wot's kids' stuff, then. If you ain't done up first!'

'Get away: just you and some woman. I know what you want to do.'

'You bloody don't, mate! Listen: soon's you open up that 'ut, I get the mob up, see? An' they get the ladders out of the 'ut an' they're up on the church roof, see, gettin' the lead orf. Then we get the lead in under the tents and 'ide it and then orf we go an' no one knows, see? The mob comes back p'raps a week or two later wiv a van, busts open the 'ut, scarpers wiv the lot.'

'But why can't they bring their own ladders?'

'Stoopid! If you was a copper an' you saw some blokes marchin' through the streets late at night carrying a ladder, wot would you think?'

Royston nodded.

'See, jus' the same, if you saw a van outside a church an' the next day you 'eard the lead was orf the roof, you'd remember the van, wouldn't yer? But you wouldn't remember a van if it was a week later.'

'It's a very good plan.'

'S'mine, as a matter o' fack,' said Tod, studying his finger nails.

'Who else is in it?'

'Terry and Les; Gerry Connell and Joey Zimbara. I'm the leader, see, the master-mind.'

Royston was silent for a while. He felt considerably sobered; a bit of a lark was one thing, but this sounded very wrong indeed. 'Well, I dunno –'

'Are you turning yeller, you little –?'

'No, but –'

'Windy, aren't yer? Wanna be good, wanna grow up a goody-goody, wanna be like ole fat-gut Woodington, wanna work in a fact'ry for two measly quid a week. Soft, that's you, softy!'

'I'm not! I'm not!'

'Soft-guts Beedman!'

'I'm not! I'm not Beedman! I'm – I want –'

A passing train gave him a moment to think. Tod casually threw a stone at it.

'All right, Tod; I'll do it for you, but listen, I want you to do something for me.'

'Ah, shut up!'

'No, listen, Tod, will you? What's this place at Chipham you're going to?'

'Why?'

'I want to know.'

'It's a foster-'ome, I told yer. Some ole bag who takes boys in.'

'Would she have room for me?'

'You're not coming muckin' up my lodge, mate; you find one of your bloody own.'

'Listen, Tod, I must get to Chipham; I've got something to do there. Would your old woman take me in?'

'Well, yeah; as a matter of fack she 'as got room for two. She arsked me if I'd like to bring along a littel mate in case I got lonely. Littel mate! Cor! What yer goin' to do for money?'

'I only want a few days there, I hope. I can pay that out of the pound I get for this job.'

'I'll want ten bob for introducin' yer.'

'You won't get it!' Royston felt like punching the other boy between the eyes. Tod flinched but stuck to his guns. 'I shan't give yer the old girl's address, then.'

'Oh, all right. I've got some money saved up for camp, I'll pinch it out of the office.'

'Cor! You reelly goin' on the loose again, Roy?' It was Tod's turn to feel an unwilling admiration: even he had not attempted breaking into Mr Woodington's office and then absconding with the cash-box. 'Wot ever for?'

'I want to find my mother.'

'Wot the 'ell for? You stoopid great twit! Wot ever good will that do?'

'I've got to know who she is!'

'Wot's it matter 'oo she is? She's let yer down, same as mine 'as. It doesn't matter 'oo she was, you can't get over that. You're on yer own, mate; you grab wot yer can, an' the best o' British luck!'

'I'm going to find out.'

'You can't, you soppy date! The Gov'ment'll stop yer.'

'How?'

'They will. They're all the bloody same, they're all against yer. They call yer Beedman all the time, don't they? Well, then! Grab wot yer can while yer can, mate, and sod 'em.'

'Oh, you don't understand, Tod. At least, not all of it. If I can't find her I'll look after myself, like you say; there's nobody here will help me, I know that; I might as well finish with the lot of them.'

'But wot yer goin' to do for money? I ain't goin' to give yer none.'

'I'll do something. Pinch something perhaps. I could get a job; I'm nearly fifteen. I could say I was older.'

'Yer can't, not wivout cards.'

'What cards?'

'Insurance. You can't get a job wivout cards.'

This was a new one to Royston; he began to see what he was up against. There was a long silence. He began to waver: perhaps it would be better to wait till he was fifteen and could get these vital cards. Then Tod made up his mind. He had no sympathy with Royston, but he was far more apprehensive than he showed over his forthcoming change of lodgings and move to a strange new town. Royston would be company of sorts; Royston might give him some sort of help if the police came after him for this lead-stealing job; and finally if Royston went on the loose for some time there might be a reward offered for his recovery. Yes. 'Aw right, Roy,' he said. 'You're goin' to be there Wednesday, aincha? Joey'll carve you up if you ain't.'

'Yes, I'll be there, Tod.'

'Aw right. Mrs Burge, forty-seven Ash Street, Chipham. When will you be there?'

'When are you going, Tod?'

'Friday morning. Ole Archer's takin' me over.'

Royston considered, eyes darting about the mossy roof of the gun-post, fingers drumming nervously on his knee. Then he said, with a sudden catch in his throat: 'All right, then. Tell her I'll be there Friday night.'

13

IT was raining – a steady, seeping, light rain that seemed almost like mist when you looked across the meadow; a rain that did not patter on the foliage, but made its presence obvious by the great pearly blobs on the dock leaves and the bending of the grass under the weight of moisture. It was a silent world, cowering under the low grey clouds. The thorn trees were drenchd with wet, but stood motionless as there was no wind. Deep in the heart of the hedge no rain fell, but the earth was damp, sucking water horizontally as if it was brown blotting-paper. Royston lay there like a dead body, huddled on the earth with his head pillowed on his little weekend bag. He was fast asleep.

He was a rare type of absconder: he had prepared for his getaway without giving any hint to the other children. To begin with, he had sensed rather than worked out intellectually that Mr Woodington had his eye on his visits to that distant corner of the shrubbery which, over the past year, he had silently and fiercely established as his own; but he went there for neither of the reasons Mr Woodington thought he did – he went there to be alone. Now it became suddenly a place he could use as part of his plan. He found a cache in another part of the garden, actually in the orchard on the other side of a loose board in the fence; and then, whenever he felt Mr Woodington's eye upon him, he would go across to the shrubbery and stay there five minutes, both long enough and short enough to attract attention. The Superintendent became curious; one day while Royston was at school he went across to the shrubbery and had a good look round, even poking into the gloomy earth; but he found nothing. He did not think to look anywhere else.

It was not easy for Royston to smuggle the week-end bag out into the new cache, for there were a lot of eyes at Hawthorn

Hill – nineteen other kids and four staff – and the movements of all of them were unpredictable. Royston managed it in three stages – out to the laundry in a pile of soiled sheets, from the laundry to the back of the coke store when he filled the staff scuttle, and then along the fence to the gap during the evening. Clothes were much easier : he could walk out of the house wearing them under his day-clothes, and there was no clothing check between Monday and Thursday. In this way he packed away a complete change of garments and extra socks and pants; his mac he pretended to leave at school on the Wednesday.

He soon decided that to get money from the locked cash-box in Mr Woodington's locked office was quite impossible. There was, however, enough money for his needs in the secretary's office at school, and it was easy for him on the Wednesday to leave one window in the boys' lavatories closed but not latched. He knew he could find his way round the school in the dark without using lights.

On the Wednesday evening he set out for the Boys' Brigade wearing his best clothes, as was normal, with the uniform belt, pouch, and cap. Half-way through the evening he complained of stomach-ache but pretended to struggle on gamely; at length he asked permission to visit the lavatory, and Mr Price sympathetically said he could go home if he wished.

Royston got in under the pile of rolled tents in the Camp Store and lay there quite comfortably, listening to the increasing rowdiness of the meeting, smiling to himself at the shouts by well-known voices, holding his breath when it came to the quiet time for prayers at the end, and then hearing the boots clump out of the hut and the voices die away down the drive. Mr Price, humming a hymn-tune, had a quick look round, peeped into the lavatory, and then went out, slamming the door and rattling it to see if the Yale lock held. Then his footsteps, too, died away and Royston's last mooring-line parted. This time he felt no regret about it, nor was his heart thumping, nor indeed did he feel any emotion; this time his course of action extended before him in a series of stages, and it was only a case of working through them one by one. He sat up on the rolled tents, watching the watery moon and listening to the cold wind soughing through the trees about him, and waited for Tod's signal.

Why Tod had chosen an owl-call as the signal, when he could no more imitate an owl than he could a penguin, was unaccountable; presumably he had seen some similar incident at the pictures. At any rate, Royston was presently thrown into a fright by an eerie rushing noise that appeared to encircle the hut, and he had no idea it was Tod until there was a loud banging on the door and a voice yelled: 'Wake up, you stoopid B! You deaf?'

Royston opened the door and in came Tod and a drunken Irishman; they got the ladder out somehow, giggling wildly and catching the electric light a smashing blow. Royston did not follow them – he had his own task. There was in the hut what was called the canteen, which was actually a sort of dresser with locked doors. He got the little key from its hook inside the kitchen cupboard and filled his pockets with bars of chocolate; he also found some six shillings in coppers and took that. There seemed to be a lot of noise going on from the church; thin cries were coming out of the windy darkness overhead and somebody put his foot through a stained-glass window. Presently Tod came running back: 'A rope! Getta rope!' he cried. In the darkness his eyes were glittering from a flushed, excited face; Royston helped him knot guy-ropes together until they had an adequate length.

There was a frightful splintering noise coming from the church roof: Royston grew alarmed – if this went on the whole neighbourhood would be aroused and his plans ruined. He went across to the church. One of the men was leaning in the porch, idly carving his initials on the stonework.

'How's it going?' asked Royston, trying to be nonchalant.

'Awright,' said the man.

'I wonder if I could – could possibly have my money so that I could go?'

'You'll go when you're told, matey; you stop there just where you are and if you let out a squeak, I'll –' and he wagged his long, sharp thumbnail just below Royston's eye. 'And what's all this about money, what you talking about?'

'But Tod said –'

'Tod says too damned much. There's no money going around here, son. Sorry, you got it all wrong : we're just here for evening prayers,' said the man, as somebody aloft dropped a hammer through a skylight.

There was a long silence. Royston stood there miserably : bolt for it with what he had got? Or stick it out on the off-chance that he wasn't wasting time?

Suddenly the man said : 'Where you from, anyway, son? I ain't seen you around.'

'I'm from the Children's Home at Hawthorn Hill.'

'You're in a *'Ome*? You pore little mucker. 'Aven't you got no parents?'

'No.'

'Cor! Stone me. That's rough, that is. Cor, what a thing to happen to anyone. 'Ere, what did Tod say about money?'

'He said he'd give me a quid.'

'Measly swine. Here, mate, here's a couple of quid, now scarper back to the 'Ome.'

'*Thank* you, sir.'

'And here, mate, listen : if ever you're in any sort of trouble, any sort of a jam, don't you hesitate to come to me. Don't you hesitate. I'd help anybody out of one o' them places.'

'Thank you very much, sir.'

'Dance, my name is, Terry Dance. Don't you hesitate. All right, Joey, I got 'er!' he called, as a large roll of lead descended on the end of the rope and bounced deafeningly against a drain-pipe.

Royston flitted away into the darkness.

It was midnight when he got back to Hawthorn Hill : he could hear the chimes. The Home was in darkness except for the kitchen, from the large windows of which light streamed. Inside he could see Mrs Woodington moving about, clad in a dingy quilted dressing-gown, and he realized that he had never before seen her in such attire; he didn't know she ever did look like this. Her hair was all screwed up in braids, too. Suddenly, with a rush of fear, came the thought that if she was still up it probably meant that Mr Woodington was out searching for him. Hastily he backed away on all fours into the next-door garden.

Hardly had he found cover than the Woodingtons' boxer dog, Carlos, came snortling down the hill and bounded about on its great pads within a few feet of Royston's nose. The boy's blood pumped hoarsely through his ears and his skin seemed turned to polythene. But Mr Woodington sauntered unknowingly past and the dog followed him into the house. For a long time Royston watched the man and his wife sipping cocoa in the kitchen. And then at last the bedroom light went on and the kitchen light went out and then the bedroom light went out, but it was a long half-hour after that before Royston moved through the darkness and retrieved his bag.

His eight-mile march to Francombe, by the feeble light of the moon and with a light rain blowing into his face, was almost without incident. His only bad moments came when the occasional car or all-night lorry swept along the road, but almost always he had time to duck into cover; the only time he was transfixed by the headlights the driver swept past, apparently indifferent. It was just past four on a horrible grey morning when he reached the overgrown hedge and crept inside. He ate two bars of chocolate and soon afterwards fell asleep.

He awoke feeling rather damp but by no means miserable, and lay there comfortably on his back nibbling chocolate and waiting for a clock to strike so that he could tell the time. Long afterwards he heard a faint swirling clink and realized that sound was not carrying through the rain – at least not well enough for him to tell the time accurately. He lay there pondering and recalled a scene from a radio thriller he had once heard; with this in mind he made a new plan. He emerged carefully from the hedge and took his time brushing his clothes down and doing his hair, since he did not want to arouse suspicion by his appearance; then he went down to the phone box on the corner of Tebbutts Road and rang the Beedman number. He listened for a long time, but there was no reply. The coast was clear.

He had realized that ever since he left Hawthorn Hill he had met not a single pedestrian and he worked out that the miserable weather was probably keeping everybody indoors. He therefore walked quite openly and boldly round to Twelvetrees and down the well-known drive. It was a peculiar sensation. He had expected to feel all kinds of romantic sensations; he had even dreamt that the front door would fly open and a joyous figure with outstretched arms would rush towards him. But nothing happened, and nothing meant anything to him. In an emotional vacuum he walked round the side of the house. He knew they left the back door unlocked, and so it was; he went inside and wiped his shoes carefully on the mat, as he had been trained to do. Then he went swiftly and silently through the kitchen and the hall, making for the bedroom and that wardrobe where the documents, the precious clues, were kept. Half-way across the hall he stopped dead.

It was all different.

They didn't have a hallstand. His father never wore a bowler. They would never have put that old carpet down in the hall. He rushed into the lounge. It was all different: what was a piano doing there, and the carpet looked seedy. *Books* all over the place? And that settee – he stood stock still in a blizzard of fear. Over the back of the settee was slung a child's cherry-coloured blazer.

And at that moment a key rattled in the front-door lock. ...

'Bernardsgreen two-one-two.'

'Oh, hallo, Mr Woodington: David Stokes here.'

'Ah, Mr Stokes! Good! I'm glad you've rung.'

'I'm sorry if I'm late, Mr Woodington, but I've only just had your message. I've only just got in from Court. What's the trouble?'

'Beedman.'

'I'm so sorry, I didn't get that; this line is awfully noisy.'

'It's Royston Beedman, Mr Stokes: he's on the loose again.'

'Oh lord, no, really? When?'

'Last night. He went to B.B. with the other lads and while he was there he complained of stomach-ache. He was allowed to leave the parade and he hasn't been seen since. That would be about – oh, half past eight last night.'

'I see.'

'I had a scout round myself when we realized what had happened, and I informed the local bobbies at half past ten.'

'Quite right. Is there any reason you know of to make him go like this?'

'None whatever. We can't understand it. I've had a long chat with the staff, of course: there's not been a single untoward incident, no rows, no arguments; he's been as good as gold for months. We simply can't account for this.'

'Have you checked the hospitals? I suppose it's just possible he might have got an appendix flare-up and somebody found him?'

'I haven't done that, and I will do so, Mr Stokes, of course. But I think we shall draw a blank. There's a weekend bag missing and also some of his clothes, so we think the boy had this all planned. But why on earth he should go off like this I just can't fathom.'

'Oh lord!'

There was a pause.

'Might he have gone to Miss Mole?'

'I thought of that, naturally, but she's not on the phone herself and I didn't want the police to go up there frightening her.'

'I'll ask Miss Strachan to check.'

'I dunno, I'm sure.'

'Look, er, Mr Woodington, I've got a bit of a glimmer about what's in his mind, though I haven't a clue where he may be heading. I'll make a few inquiries from up here and let you know if I get any news. Will you ring me at once if you get any?'

'Yes, sure. Lord, what a life, eh? Fair turns you up, these kids.'

Mr Stokes rang off and sat fidgeting. He had given up smoking the day before but he now decided to start again. He rang Miss Strachan at East Whixham and asked her urgently to visit Miss Mole; then he went to report to his chief.

'Well, he'll turn up when he's hungry,' said Miss Kelpie, philosophically. 'They always do.'

'I'm worried about this one,' said Stokes, and told her his theory.

'Well, yes, it's possible, they do very often try and find their parents at this age, as we know. But so what? He hasn't a cat-in-hell's chance of finding her.'

'All the same, I'm damned worried.'

'But why, David? He'll wander about and then the police will find him and that'll be that. He's fifteen, he won't come to much harm.'

'It's not Royston I'm worried about, Miss Kelpie,' Stokes said gravely. 'It's that poor wretched mother of his. . . .'

Royston went into the lounge and out through the french windows like a rocketing pheasant; dragged his mac up over his head so that he wouldn't be recognized, scuttled round the house, and then fairly raced up the drive, down the lane, across the meadow, and in under the hedge, flinging himself on the earth and gasping loudly for breath. For half an hour he lay there writhing, drumming his knotted fists, cursing, weeping, in a pandemonium of fright, frustration, and anger. For a further half-hour he sat still and stony. At the end of that time he had himself under control again. He glared out bleakly at the sodden meadow.

When he had had more chocolate his mind began to work again. The afternoon had already moved into a deeper shade of grey when he emerged, brushed himself down, and went back to Tebbutts Road. He rang the Beedman number, a distracted female voice answered.

'Please could I speak to Mrs Beedman?' asked Royston politely.

'Speaking. *Who?* Oh, Mrs Beedman. I'm sorry, she doesn't live here now.'

'Oh. Oh dear. Please could you tell me where she's gone?'

'They went to Melwich about six months ago. Do you want her telephone number?'

'Er – er –' said Royston wildly.

'Oh look, I don't know her number just this minute, but she'll be in the book. It's Fifty Cedar Drive, have you got that?'

'Yes.'

'You can look it up in the book. Who is it calling?'

Royston rang off.

Melwich: now where the hell was that? Somewhere in South London, that was about all he knew. He went back to the meadow and got his bag and then trudged down to the main road, avoiding the Old Town in case someone recognized him. About a mile along the main road he picked up a Green Line coach, all fuggy and smelling of wet warm raincoats.

The conductor was quite helpful when Royston said he wanted to get to Melwich: he worked out two routes and finally set the boy down in the suburbs with the relevant bus numbers written on a piece of paper. It was now dark and the streets were slimy with rain; at the road-junction the red neon shop-signs shone cheerfully across the empty pavements. Royston had no difficulty in finding a steamy café, where he ate eggs, chips, and a slice.

When he resumed his journey he felt pleased to be plunged once again into the great anonymity of the metropolis, and at the same time frightened because he was going into unknown country. This latter feeling grew almost unbearably strong when he was at last deposited in Melwich and found he hadn't a clue about his next move.

He asked no policemen – he was steering very clear of them – and there were few other people about; but gradually he was directed towards his objective and at last turned into Cedar Drive at about nine o'clock. It was a bleak spot, high up and catching the rain-swept wind; occasional dim street-lamps flickered between the boughs of the sentinel trees.

Number Fifty was in darkness.

Royston sat on a low garden wall on the other side of the street and studied the situation. He knew that if his 'parents' were in they would be throwing a party, and if they were out they would be out for a long time; it looked as though he had a clear run now. The next house on the left had lights on downstairs, but that on the right was also dark. He decided to make his approach from the right, but he saw that he would have to go extremely cautiously. He had no torch and no matches and the moon was behind cloud; even on a clear night he could see that the black trees would shadow that side of the house. Well, it would have to be step by step. An idea occurred to him, and with a gasp of pleasure he took off his shoes and left them, with his bag, behind the wall he sat on.

It was the slowest, but the easiest, house-breaking Royston had ever done. He took a quarter of an hour to creep down the side of the house, but there were no milk bottles, no dustbins, no coke, and the back door was open. In a mounting fever of excitement he went up the stairs in a gloom filled with the secret sound of clocks.

When he got into the bedroom his resolution was almost knocked out of him. He had not been prepared for the flooding associations of scent. He stood as still as stone in the whispering dark while his 'mother's' scent brought wave upon wave of loneliness, fearfulness, helplessness, smallness and self-pity washing over him. His eyes closed; he did not think he could go on among the scents that meant so much and meant so little.

At last he moved. He felt his way across to the wardrobe. He reached up amongst the rustling dresses for the shelf at the top.

14

ADOPTION ORDER

in respect of an infant named

Royston Carter Beedman (formerly Christopher Hook)

IN THE COUNTY OF RINTINGHAM

Petty Sessional Division of Chipham

Before the Juvenile Court sitting at Chipham the Sixteenth day of November 1942

Application has been made by Gilbert Everard Beedman (hereinafter called the male applicant) a person not under the age of 25 years by occupation Company Director resident at 17 Abbey Ponds Road Chipham in England and domiciled in England and by Christine Brenda Beedman his wife (hereinafter called the female applicant) being a person not under the age of 25 years that they are desirous of being authorized under the Adoption of Children Act 1926 to adopt Royston Carter an infant of the male sex aged six months, resident at 17 Abbey Ponds Road Chipham in England, a British subject who has never been married the child of Violet Hook (herein called the infant);

And the male and female applicants being respectively not less than 21 years older than the infant;

And all the consents required by the Act having been obtained or dispensed with;

It is adjudged that the statements made in the application are true;

And it is ordered that the applicants be authorized to adopt the infant;

And as regards Costs it is ordered that the applicants do pay to the Clerk of the Justices for the said Petty Sessional Division of Chipham the sum of eight shillings.

And it is directed that the Registrar General shall make in the

Adopted Children Registrar an entry recording the adoption in accordance with the particulars set out in the Schedule to this Order.

And it having been proved to the satisfaction of the Court that the infant was born on the date mentioned and is identical with Christopher Hook to whom an entry numbered 1127 and made on the Fifteenth day of May 1942 in the Register of Births for the Registration District of Chipham and Sub-District of Chipham, in the County of Rintingham relates, it is further directed that the Registrar General shall cause the aforesaid entry in the Registrar of Births to be marked with the word 'adopted'.

ELSPETH M. DODD
Justice of the Peace for the County of
Rintingham

Royston first read over this document, which all night had seemed to be burning a hole in his pocket, while he was huddled in the corner of a shelter in Allenby Gardens. It was a moment of tense solemnity. He had unfolded the document with hands that trembled violently, as though he were opening Pandora's box. What was he to be, the son of a lord, a mayor, a foreign potentate, an American Negro? And here it was, the moment of truth: he was plain Christopher Hook, son of Violet Hook. It was a strange, unlooked-for sensation to find that his origins sounded unworthily vulgar. He felt as though a shadow had fallen on him, a queer *white* shadow, in which it slowly dawned on him that he did not feel like a Christopher, he still felt like Royston: Christopher was a measly, meagre name that had nothing to do with him, and his whole personality was built round the sound of the other name. The longer he stared at the Order, the less he felt that it had anything to do with him; and yet it had, for that infant was indubitably him. The few crisp outlines of his life suddenly slithered into mist; it was as though he had spent all these years in the fortress of his skin and suddenly someone had flung open the Traitor's Gate. Hook, he hung on to that, Hook, it sounded blunt and down-to-earth, safe in a way; Royston Hook, yes, that fitted better, he could wear that, it didn't sound bad. Royston Hook: he tested out the name aloud. Yes, not bad; and at least better than that detestable, repulsive name of Beedman, which had never seemed to fit.

Eight bob! That was the price they paid for him, a mingy eight bob! Fury shook him for some minutes, to think that he, he of all people, had been bandied about from hand to hand at the cut-rate price of two packets of fags! And the whole transaction written down on a tatty old bit of paper not much better than a County Council Order Form! Of all the undignified scrambles, what the hell was this woman, this Violet Hook, thinking of to let it happen to him, what cruel monster was she to toss away her own flesh and blood for – for two weeks' pocket money? The *bitch*!

When his fury cooled again, he saw that eight shillings was actually the price of the name Beedman, and that wasn't worth any more. Indeed, if he could somehow reverse the process and get rid of the hated name for eight bob, it would be cheap at the price. This was a heartening thought : eight bob was well within his means. Carefully he folded the Adoption Order with fingers that seemed to have become swollen with emotion. Then he tidied himself up, sluiced his face at the drinking-fountain, and emerged into Melwich High Gate.

It was now half past seven on the Friday morning. The rain had stopped, and the puddles in the streets reflected the bright blue of the sky. Royston went along High Gate until, by the Southern Electric station, he found a scruffy little café frequented by taxi-men, where he got a breakfast of sausages and baked beans.

He had spent the night in a greenhouse, in a garden about a hundred yards from the Beedman house. It had been warm and dry, but he had slept poorly, waking every few minutes in acute apprehension in case he had overslept and now lay exposed to the hostile world. Fortunately the dawn, flooding strangely into his bedroom, had awoken him in good time; he spent a terrified minute escaping from the garden under those blank day-lit windows, feeling hugely conspicuous. But nothing happened. He buttoned up his mac and walked briskly down to the town centre, and the only person he saw was a sleepy policeman pedalling to work.

Mr Stokes got out his car and drove over to Melwich first thing in the morning. On the way he thought about Royston. He was not entirely convinced that he knew what the boy was trying to do, but he was fairly sure he did; Miss Mole now knew him best, and she *was* sure. Mr Stokes wanted to try and find the boy's mother. If the boy did trace her, Mr Stokes could perhaps get there first and prepare her. If the boy was picked up by the police first, Mr Stokes could at least talk to him about his mother and perhaps even exorcize this maternal spectre from his mind. It was strange that he had not been picked up yet; not that the police were likely to spot him, for the circularized description was very ordinary and it could have fitted thousands, but it was odd that the boy had been able to subsist for two nights without drawing attention to himself. Mr Stokes feared that Royston must be stealing to keep himself going.

He trod on his brakes suddenly and cursed as a bus pulled out right in front of him. He did not see Royston on the upper deck.

When he got to the Beedman house, the door was opened by the daily woman. 'Ooh, sir, Mrs Beedman's not at 'ome.'

'Is she sleeping off that party last night?'

'Yes! Cor, sir, no, I reelly can't say.'

'Give her my compliments and say I'd like to see her urgently.'

The daily came back with a spot of red on each cheek. 'She sez – er – well, that she's not seeing anyone, sir.'

'Tell her she can see me now or the police later – she can please herself.'

After a pause, Mr Stokes heard the bed-spring twang furiously overhead. Mrs Beedman came down in a yellow housecoat; she looked white and terrible.

'Have you no manners at all?' she stormed.

'No,' said Mr Stokes coldly.

'Oh, it's you!' she said, getting him into focus. 'Oh God, what now?'

'Has Royston been here?'

'Do you mean to tell me you've forced me out of bed to talk about *him*? Get out of my house, get out, get out!'

128

'Has he been here?'

'Will you go or shall I call the police?' she said, lurching towards the phone.

'I've told you, you can talk to me or you can talk to the police; please yourself. Has Royston been here?'

'Do you think he'd show his nose within a mile of this place? Gilbert'd bash hell out of him if he did, and he knows it. So would I. Gladly. After all the trouble he's caused, coming between me and my – why are you asking this?'

'Royston's missing.'

'Good! *You're* having trouble! Good! That'll show you. It wasn't just us, was it? Eh? Poor misunderstood little thing, you all thought. Well, you're finding out the truth about him now, aren't you?'

'No,' said Mr Stokes.

He offered her a cigarette. She refused it haughtily: she looked like a horse whose stable is on fire.

'I want some information, Mrs Beedman.'

'Then you can ask for it somewhere else,' she said.

'I can get a subpoena.'

'We've got a good lawyer too.'

'I dare say. I thought you might like to avoid the expense.'

For a moment he thought she was going to face him out, and he was scared: he had wildly exceeded his authority. Then she shouted: 'Mrs Gregory! Bring me some coffee!' and to him: 'I'll have that cigarette now.'

When she'd got her coffee, she said: 'Make it snappy, then.'

'You adopted that boy at Chipham?'

'I told you that.'

'What was the exact date?'

'How the hell should I know?'

'How old was he?'

'Oh Christ, I don't know. About six months.'

'What was the mother's name?'

'Butcher. Or Baker. Or Candlestick-maker, what does it matter?'

'Was she a local girl? Have you ever seen her since?'

'God, no! We don't hobnob with people of that class. Who do you think we are – Do you want to find her?'

'I do.'

'Was there something wrong with the adoption?' He could tell by the gleam in her eyes that she was thinking of suing the County Council for all those years' parental contributions.

'There was not.'

'You just want to find her. You just innocently want to find her. All right. Go ahead. Go ahead and find her. Tell her from me she's welcome to what she's going to get. And I'll tell you something else; from now on, Gil and I don't pay one penny piece for that little tramp. What? When you're going behind our backs taking him back to his *mummy*? Not a penny piece. Sue us. Take us to Court. See what we'll say –'

'That's enough, Mrs Beedman. I'd like to have full particulars of the boy's birth, please.'

'Listen: upstairs I've got all the papers about that business – God knows why I kept them. You can have them. You can have them with my compliments. You can do what the hell you like with them. As far as I'm concerned, as from now they're cancelled. Finished. The lot.'

She swept out and he heard her go banging up the stairs; he winced as he thought of what it must be doing to her head. There was a silence and then he heard her come much more slowly down.

'Everything's been taken,' she said. 'And this was on the floor by the window.'

She held out a clean and neatly-folded handkerchief. Along one hem was printed in smudgy marking-ink: 'HAWTHORN'.

They looked at each other. For entirely different reasons, both their faces had become quite stony. . . .

Chipham Juvenile Court was a brown-brick building that looked and smelt like a museum. Royston had tripped jauntily up the steps, but then he stopped, petrified: the place was packed with policemen! And, by one of those momentary quirks of fortune, they were all at that instant staring solemnly at him! It was only because his muscles had frozen that he did not bolt out madly into the traffic. Instead, he turned jerkily and stumbled off down the street, and in this way found himself pausing for breath by a doorway marked with a painted sign: Hamilton, Tonks, Solicitors. Commissioners of Oaths. Clerk to the Justices.

Clerk to the Justices: now, this must be the geezer who'd got the eight bob that made him Beedman. Royston went in and climbed an extremely dark, steep stairway, at the top of which he found himself facing a small counter, a telephone switch-board, and a girl with supercilious make-up.

She looked up from her nails with eyebrows lifted.

'Can I speak to the manager?' said Royston hoarsely.

The girl expressed Olympian amusement that made him feel he was eighteen inches high and covered with mud.

'Do you want Mr Tonks or Mr Dunwoodie?' she asked.

'I dunno,' said Royston.

The girl closed her eyes, tilted her head, and lifted one shoulder: 'Oh, well, if you haven't that much brain, Ay can't help you, can Ay?'

Royston stood and stared balefully at her. The girl attempted to resume filing her nails, but she was evidently discomposed and presently she picked up her telephone and said: 'Mr Crawley: there's a – a person here –'

The telephone barked and as she replaced it a door opened right beside Royston, making him nearly jump out of his skin, and out came a small, silver-haired man with an experienced face. He seemed surprised by Royston's age. 'Yes, my lad?'

'Are you the manager?' asked Royston, nervousness making him boorish.

'I'm the chief clerk; will I do?'

'Yes,' said Royston.

He was ushered into a tiny cubicle containing two chairs; as the door closed behind him he heard the telephone girl heave a resigned sigh. He blushed.

'Now, what's the trouble, lad?'

'I want to find something out,' blurted Royston.

'Oh yes. What sort of something?'

Royston fidgeted about. He didn't know where to begin. He

felt like an idiot. Then he remembered his manners. 'I'm very sorry to trouble you, sir,' he said.

'That's all right, son.'

Royston considered again. 'Well, you see, sir, I'm an adopted boy.'

'Oh, yes.'

'It's rather a complicated story, sir, only you see – well, what's happened is that, well, the people that adopted me, they've sort of – well they've died. And what I want to do is find – well, my real mother.'

'Yes.'

'I came here, sir, because you see the adoption was done here.'

Royston dived into his inside pocket and produced the adoption order. Mr Crawley glanced cursorily at it and said : 'I see.'

'Well – I – thought p'raps you could help me, sir.'

'Quite so.'

The voice was kind, but the man was being absolutely no help. Royston mumbled on a bit longer, then fell silent. His eyes flickered uneasily round the cubicle, his face went a deep crimson, he hung his head.

After looking at him kindly for a while, Mr Crawley sighed and said : 'I'm sorry, son, I'm very sorry, but I can't help you at all. I'm simply not allowed to : the law won't let me divulge any information whatever about your mother. It won't let me and it won't let anybody else help you either. You see, your mother has what we call relinquished all parental rights over you; as far as you're concerned, in law she simply does not exist any more.'

Royston raised his head. His face was still crimson and tears were brimming along his eyelids. Mr Crawley leant forward and patted his knee. 'Look at it this way, lad – you're a sensible chap, I can see that. It often happens – not necessarily in your case, I'm not saying that, but often – that a girl who's very young, too young to be married, slips up and has a baby; you know how it can happen I expect – you must talk about such things among yourselves. Sometimes it happens that the father of the baby is a soldier or sailor who perhaps gets killed in battle before he can get leave to marry. Now, what's the girl to do? She wants to do the best thing for her baby, because they love their babies, these girls, believe me. But what is she to do? She knows she can't marry, she knows she's got to go out to work to earn money for herself, and she knows she can't look after the baby as tenderly as she wants to. So she finally decides that the best thing she can do for her baby, to help him, is to entrust him to people who are in a position to bring him up for her and look after him lovingly and kindly.'

'They're not at all like that!' cried Royston, his chin jerking.

'Oh, come now, I think they are; I think if you're honest with yourself you'll admit that they are. However, be that as it may, the baby's mother tries to do the best she can to give her child love and security, which is most important, to my mind. And then very likely she grows a little older and marries a nice young fellow and they start a family of their own.'

'And she forgets all about the baby!' cried Royston bitterly.

'Oh no; oh no, she never forgets him, but she comforts herself with the thought that she did what was best for her baby at the time.'

'Then when the time's past, why doesn't she have him back if she loves him?'

'Think how upsetting that would be! The child has learnt to love the adoptive parents, and the adoptive parents have learnt to love him, and the children of the marriage don't want a strange brother suddenly arriving, do they? Think what you'd feel; and the mother's husband, well, he hasn't had anything to do with the first baby, how do we know that he will love the baby just as he ought to? No, the law says that things must stay as they are, and the law is very wise in that, isn't it?'

Royston gave a half-stifled grunt. There was an uneasy silence. Royston was deep in misery, visualizing the end of his quest, the ignominious creeping back – somewhere – nothing solved. Mr Crawley was not certain what to do with this obviously unconvinced and drooping figure. Relief came in the shape of an acne-studded youth who popped his head round the door and said: 'S'cuse me, Mr Crawley, will you have your coffee in here?'

'No, I'll come through, Michael. Er, Michael, would there be an extra cup of coffee in the pot this morning?'

'Yeah. Can do.'

'Bring one to this lad will you?' They went out together and Royston heard Mr Crawley say, in the corridor: 'Sit with him while he drinks it, will you, son? He's a bit upset but he'll soon be over it. Then see him off.'

Michael brought the coffee back. Royston accepted his gratefully. After a bit, Michael said: 'What's to do with you, then?'

'Oh. Fed up.'

'Don't be like that. The world is young, never say die and all that claptrap, what?'

Royston was silent.

'What's up, then? Gendarmes on your track?'

'No, I just wanted to find somebody.'

'What-what-what-what-what? And won't old Creepy help you?'

'No.'

'I hear you, my little wooden capitaine. Major Bloodnock at your service: on receipt of your photograph of a cheque, I will personally take up a photograph of your case. Ay theng you!' Michael imitated the sound of a cash-register and various other 'Goon Show' noises; it wasn't bad, and Royston smiled involuntarily and told Michael what he was after. Michael listened attentively.

'Yes-yes-yes,' he said, when Royston had finished. 'The plot sickens. Know what I'd do if I were you, old man?'

'What?'

'We can't help you here; old Creepy's quite right, it's not allowed. But if I were you I'd go up to Somerset House.'

'What's that?'

'Where all the birth certificates are – up West, in the Strand. Now if you was to go there and get your birth certificate, your real one, it'd show you where you were born and your mother's address; and then, if you went to that address, ten to one you'd find someone who remembered your mum.'

'Cor! Thanks! I'll do that!'

'And the best of British luck.'

'I say, er, do I owe you a fee?'

'Certainly, sah : two million pounds, or I'll settle for a photograph of Queen Victoria. Don't be daft! Go on, on your way. Green Line from the Bus Station, get out at Trafalgar Square.'

Royston picked up his bag and parted gratefully from his helpful friend. He emerged into the High Street five seconds after Mr Stokes had gone into the Probation Office, next door.

15

AFTER he left Mrs Beedman, Mr Stokes drove to Chipham and called at the police-station. He said he thought Royston might be wandering around in Chipham.

'Oh, ah?' said the desk-sergeant cheerfully. 'I'll ask the man on the High Street to keep a weather-eye open.'

Stokes thanked him and crossed the main road to the Area Children's Office. He knew the woman in charge, Miss King-Dean, slightly; they met at conferences and here and there.

'I'm afraid most of the adoption records are kept at County Hall,' said Miss King-Dean. 'Unless it's a very recent one?'

'The end of forty-two, I think; possibly early in forty-three.'

'Oh, no, then, I can't help you at all. Nor could County Hall, I should think. Anyway, you don't want to go all that way, I suppose? What's it all about?'

Stokes told her.

'What a fascinating case! Look I should try the Divisional Health Office; they've got all those old Health Visitors' cards stacked away there, and I dare say they could trace the whole thing.'

'What's your Magistrates' Clerk like?'

'Old Tonks. Bit of a stickler; very fair, but sticky.'

'He wouldn't open his files to me?'

'He's not allowed to, surely?'

'I thought I'd read somewhere that they could give the information now if a case was made out?'

'You're thinking of the new Act, I expect; or the Hurst Report. Anyway, try old Tonks, by all means, but I should think Health's the best bet, or possibly Education – they did the guardian *ad litem* work in those days.'

Mr Stokes thanked her, and as he was going, she said: 'Oh,

by the way, David, this boy you're putting in Ash Street with Mrs Burge. You don't half poach in my area, do you?'

'It's not me! Ron Archer's putting a boy there, I think, I've vaguely heard about it.'

'Would Mrs Burge take another?'

'I've no idea.'

'I've got a kid I've got to fix up tonight,' said Miss King-Dean. 'Would you mind if I asked her?'

'Of course not. It's your area.'

'I'll stroll round there this afternoon. No harm in asking, anyhow,' she said.

Mr Stokes went up the road to the Divisional Health Office. After a long pause there came out to him a small, bald man in a wing collar. He held Mr Stokes' card in his hand and looked pained. 'Mr Stokes? I think you want the Children's Department, sir, they deal with adoption inquiries. Number One Five Seven, High –'

'I've been there.'

'Number One Five Seven, High Street, sir, the Children's Department.'

'I've been there,' repeated Mr Stokes.

The little man looked amazed.

'Look, I'm trying to get some information about an adoption and if I could have a sight of the Health Visitors' record-cards I think that would help.'

'Oh, Health Visitors' records! Quite so. Yes, they are here. Now if you would write in –'

'This matter is pretty urgent; I'm afraid I don't want to wait for correspondence. You keep these cards well indexed and handy?'

'Oh, yes, of course. But really I should have the authority of the D.M.O. before I open up our records – they are *medical* records, you know.'

'Is the D.M.O. in?'

'I'm afraid he's not. If you would write in, or better still ask your County Medical Officer to write in –'

'I can't spare the time. Look here, the fact is –' and Mr Stokes told the story again. He was getting quite sick of it.

The little man looked as though he was having to decide whether to go to war with China.

'Well, I don't know,' he said, reluctantly producing a propelling pencil and a piece of paper. 'What was the name of the infant?'

'Beedman. B double E. Or it might be Butcher or it might be Baker.'

The little man looked not only pained but pitying. 'We have a very great number of babies on our index, you know.'

'Yes, I'm sure, but if your cards are properly filed –'

'Of course they are,' said the man looking nettled. 'What was the date of the adoption order?'

'Somewhere between November '42 and say March '43.'

'1942!' The man put his pencil away. 'I'm sorry, sir, but all cards prior to 1950 are parcelled up in the basement; it would take a very considerable time –'

'But surely you've got a minion? Or look, I'll come down and look myself.'

'I'm sorry, sir, but that would not be permitted. We are very short-staffed, and I myself have a complex report to prepare for Committee next week. Your obvious course is to get your C.M.O. to write in to our D.M.O. –'

Mr Stokes flounced out.

He tried Education but they said all their early records were at County Hall, but if he would care to write in. . . .

He had a cup of coffee and a cigarette and it then dawned on him that the Probation Officers might be able to help him here. He went back down the High Street and into their squalid suite.

(Royston emerged from the Clerk's Office and crossed the road by the pedestrian crossing, while the policeman held up the traffic for him. He caught the Green Line at the station and it started immediately.)

There was only one Probation Officer in, an enthusiastic young man named Jaffa. He obligingly searched their card-index, but there was no mention of Beedman, Butcher or Baker.

'The chap you really want is my colleague, Mr Harris,' Jaffa said. 'He's been here donkey's years; he knows this town inside out. Even if he didn't handle the case himself, he'd probably have heard of it.'

'Is he in?'

'I'm awfully sorry, no. He won't be in today, he's taking a boy to an Approved School.'

'But surely he's only got to go to Redhill?'

'Ah, but he's got to fetch the boy from Winchester. I don't expect to see him today.'

'How about tomorrow?'

'It's my Saturday on, worse luck.'

'Oh God!'

'I'm terribly sorry. Look, I'll leave a note on his desk and if by any chance he gets back late this afternoon, I'll get him to ring you. Can we leave it like that?'

Moodily, Mr Stokes agreed to leave it like that. When he got back to his car, he found that the policeman in the High Street had booked him for a parking offence. . . .

Royston got to Somerset House at half past eleven and paused under the archway, overawed by the size of the vast courtyard before him. Then he noticed by his elbow a wooden notice-board saying: *Birth Certificates, Adoption Certificates, door opposite.* He crossed to the other side of the gatehouse and went in through the swing doors. A man in uniform immediately swooped on him. Royston was terrified, but the man said kindly: 'Yes, son?'

'Wanna birth stificate,' mumbled Royston.

'In there, up to the counter,' nodded the man.

Royston walked into a large room like a post office, where there was a big counter with a wire grille. One of the half-dozen men behind the grille said: 'Yes, son?'

'Birth stificate?' mumbled Royston.

'Short or long?'

Royston stared at him in perplexity.

'A short certificate costs 9d. and a long one 3s. 9d.,' explained the man. 'What you want it for, son, employment? A short one will do you.'

Royston half nodded his head and then, as the man looked

139

patient and kind, he said: 'I want to find out where I was born. And my mum's address when I was born.'

'You'll have to have a long certificate for that, son, 3s. 9d. You know when you were born, I suppose?'

'Well, it's always been May 15th,' said Royston, though rather doubtfully, for he wasn't really sure of anything.

'Then it still is, son. But if you're not certain you can always make a search.'

Royston nodded. The man looked keenly at him for a moment and then said: 'Well, I expect it'll be all right. It's an extra 1s. 6d. to make a search. Have you got the money?'

Royston looked dubious for a moment, but on putting his hand in his pocket his fingers closed on his second pound note, so he brought it out and the man said: 'Right. Go over to that desk behind you, son, and fill up a buff form, and then take it with your 1s. 6d. to my colleague along the end there.'

Royston went over and started filling up the form: 'I require ... long birth certificate(s) –' Some of the questions alarmed him. 'Father's full name; father's occupation': how the devil did he know? He looked round for help but none came, so he left those spaces blank. Mother's name: 'Violet Hook,' he wrote. Mother's maiden name. *Maiden?* In the end he wrote: 'Violet.' Signed 'Royston Hook.' Address? Oh, hell, address. Eventually he wrote in a deliberately illegible scrawl: 'Twelve-trees, Grange Rd, Francombe.'

He took his form to the man at the end of the counter, who kindly put some of the details right for him and gave Royston a compassionate look. Then he passed the form through a little receipt-printing machine and gave it back and said: 'Right. Through that door behind you, son.'

As Royston turned, he became aware for the first time that above his head were narrow galleries running round three sides of the room, and these galleries passed in front of shelves loaded with row upon row of vast red leather volumes. In a mounting fever of excitement Royston crept up the spiral stair-case on to the first gallery. It was very narrow, with reading-shelves on one side and the vast tomes on the other; Royston had to squeeze his way along between a lot of men from the insurance companies and the Salvation Army, who were banging the ledgers open and shut with weary irreverence.

He soon found the 1942 ledgers – Mar., June, Sept., Dec. – but he was born in May, where the hell was May? He looked wildly all over the shelves: there were no Mays anywhere. Then a smallish man in uniform, with big G.R.O. badges on his lapels, who was on duty on the gallery, came to his rescue, and courteously explained that each ledger dealt with a quarter of a year. 'Let's have a look at your form, son. May, yes, well, May falls in the quarter ending June '42 and it's Hook, so you want this one.' This was a mighty tome labelled 'June 1942 G–O'. There was a strong leather loop at the back of each ledger; the officer seized the loop, swung the book on to the reading-shelf with a clonk and said: 'There y'are, son, off you go.'

Royston excitedly turned the big pages. Long, long lists of names in double columns, each name followed by the mother's maiden name and the district of registration. Glover – Green – Guy – Hammond – Henderson – Honeywell – Hook, here we are, Hook Adam – Hook Bernard – Hook Bridget C – Hook Christopher J, Smith Newcastle T., that wasn't him – Hook Christopher, Hook Chipham, there he was!

Opposite this entry was written: '174A. 1127.' Now what the hell did that mean? How the hell did that help him?

'Now, son, let's have another look at you,' said the uniformed officer, reappearing.

Royston pointed mutely.

'That's right, now give us your form. Now in this last column you put Chipham 174A. 1127, see? I've done it for you. Now take your form back to the gentleman at the counter.'

Royston, still puzzled, put the 1942 ledger away and returned down another staircase, to the man behind the grille downstairs.

'Got it, have you, son? That's the way. Give us your 3s. 9d., then. Ta. Now, you want this posted to you?'

'No! Can't I have it?'

'Yes, certainly, son, come back at four o'clock, it'll be ready for you.'

'Four o'clock?' blurted Royston.

'That's right. You see, son, this number you've written down there tells us which of the big registers to look in, and then our clerks in there copy out the certificate for you, and it'll be in that tray ready at four o'clock.'

Royston thanked him and wandered off down the Strand. The long afternoon dragged by. He had a look at Charing Cross station and the river, and hurried very self-consciously past Scotland Yard, and then found a News Cinema, a new experience for him. The price of his seat shocked him, and during a more boring film he counted his money surreptitiously. Oh, not too bad, he had his coach fare back to Chipham and there'd be about five bob over: he could get fish and chips for his tea.

At four o'clock on the dot he was back in Somerset House.

'There you are, then, son. Now you're all right, eh?'

Royston thanked him very much.

He could hardly wait to get out into the archway to read the precious thing. There, standing within a few feet of the clattering Strand throng, he unfolded the document and read:

No 1127: When and where born:	Fifteenth May, 1942 The Hollies Nursing Home, Gisborne Hill, Chipham U.D.
Name, if any:	Christopher
Sex:	Male
Name and Surname of Father:	—
Name and Maiden Surname of Mother:	Violet Chastity Hook a Munition Worker
Rank or Profession of Father:	—
Signature, Description and Residence of Informant:	V. C. Hook, mother, of 7 Cottonmill Row, Chipham U.D.
When registered:	15 May 1942
Signature of Registrar:	D. Hand

Mr Stokes felt unexpectedly nettled when he returned to County Hall after lunch and found Miss Mole waiting for him.

'I'm ever so sorry to bother you, Mr Stokes, only I felt I had to hop on the bus and come over. What's happening?'

'Nothing's happening, Miss Mole, I'm up a gum-tree.'

'No news of my boy?'

'Not a clue.'

'Oh lor. Mr Stokes, you don't think he could have come to some harm, do you? Be lying in a ditch dying of exposure or something? Or run over?'

'No, I'm sure he's not,' said Mr Stokes, surprised that he hadn't thought of this. 'I don't know why I've never thought of that, but I haven't. I think he's still going strong somewhere.'

'Dear lor, what's he living on, then? It's been two days now.'

'I'm rather afraid that he's keeping himself going by stealing, Miss Mole.'

'Oh, poor little devil. What are you going to do when you find him?'

'I don't know. Miss Kelpie wants to bung him in the Remand Home; she says he needs a shaking. I'd prefer to see him go to Banns Cross myself – we can work from there. I dunno. A lot depends on what he's been up to while he's been on the loose.'

'Can't he go back to Hawthorn Hill?'

'They won't have him, Miss Mole. They're adamant. They say if he comes back after this exploit the other kids'll hero-worship him. It'll undermine their authority, they say. Besides, there's some money missing from the school.'

'Oh dear! Do they say Roy took it?'

'Nobody knows; it could be him, it could be anyone, we shall never prove anything. Come to think of it, a great deal may depend on how he answers when we ask him about that.'

'Oh dear, oh dear, oh dear! I wish there was something I could *do*.'

'There isn't anything you can do, Miss Mole. I'm sorry you've had this journey for nothing, but really the best thing to do is to go home and put your feet up, and I promise to let you know as soon as the police have picked him up.'

'I wish the police wasn't involved in this, they're so inhuman. It's a welfare thing, reelly, isn't it?'

'The police are better than I am at finding people, Miss Mole.'

'Ah, well, Mr Stokes: I'm very sorry if I seem to be a worrying old woman, but – well, there's not a bus back till five, would you mind if I just popped my head round the door about half past four, just in case you've heard something? Would you mind?'

'All right, Miss Mole. You do that. If I'm out, I'll leave a note for you.'

'No, my duck. Sorry. There ain't nobody o' that name 'ere.' Royston stared back at her mutely.

'You don't mean *Cook*, do yer? There's a Cook somewhere in the next block. I don't know 'er, mind, but I know the name.'

'No, it's definitely Hook,' said Royston.

'No, then I don't, duck. I would know if I'd 'eard it; I mean I was one of the first to move into these flats when they was built, I know nearly everybody. I mean, there's O'Mallys next door and Throckmortons next to them and upstairs there's –'

'When were the flats built?'

'Two years ago, ducks. No, I tell a lie, three years ago, that's right, because my Madeleine –'

'Oh,' said Royston. 'I see. The – er – the lady I was looking for lived here in 1942.'

'Aow! In the old 'ouse, you must mean! Oh, no wonder, then. The old 'ouse, yeah!'

'What happened to it?'

'Flying bomb, my dear. Smashed right on it. Everybody killed, so they say. 1944, that'd be. Yeah! You mean the old 'ouse, what used to be Number Seven!'

Royston picked up his bag and went slowly down the stairs of the block of council flats.

So that was it, he thought. That was flipping it. She was dead. Killed in the war. And now he'd never know what she looked like. In the Green Line coach, coming back from London, he had looked out of the window at all the women, wondering did she look like that one, blonde and bespectacled, or that little excited dark one, or that reflective grey-haired one – yes, she looked kind and unhurried, something like that, perhaps that *was* her! And now he would never know.

He turned into Battery Road. Where would she be buried? He'd have to go back to Somerset House and find out, he supposed. Oh, why bother? Still, pity to leave it all still a bit in the air. Perhaps he ought to round off his quest by finding her grave. He wasn't sure if he wanted to leave flowers there or spit on it.

What *would* she have looked like?

Here, wait a minute, this Nursing Home place, this Hollies dump: they'd have seen her, they'd have spoken with her.

He turned north again and asked his way to Gisborne Hill. . . .

'Can I speak to Mr David Stokes?'

'Mr Stokes speaking. Who is that?'

'Rints Children's Department, Area Two.'

'Oh, hallo, Miss King-Dean. Have you got my wandering boy?'

'Well, listen, I've been round to see that Mrs Burge of yours.'

'Oh yes: any luck?'

'No, and I'll tell you why. She's got that boys of yours, Tod something, or something Tod – he's been there since this morning. But she can't let me have her spare bed for my boy because she's promised it to a mate of Tod's who's arriving tonight. She doesn't know who this mate is, she's never seen him, but she gathers that his name is Roy.'

'Oho! Now, I wonder?'

'Yes, I wonder, too. Do these two striplings know each other?'

'Yes, they do. They come from the same Home. What time's this mate of Tod's arriving?'

'Later this evening, that's all she knows. She's got the bed ready for him.'

'I think I'll come over.'

'Come and have tea with me, David.'

'Well, thanks, but I don't think I can get away from here by teatime. I'll come over later. But I'll let you know how things work out. Thanks a lot for letting me know; it looks as though this may be it.'

'You're welcome. Have you got anyone over there who'd take a fifteen-year-old enuretic tonight?'

'Oh, yes, scores of foster-mothers specializing in that sort of thing. Ha, ha. Good-bye now.'

Mr Stokes put back the receiver and looked at it with distaste. He knew what he was going to do; but he didn't much like himself for doing it.

'Matron? Excuse me, Matron. There's a boy to see you, Matron.'

'A boy?'

The burly woman in blue uniform looked disbelievingly over the tops of her spectacles at the domestic who had answered the front door. She went on looking like this for a full half-minute; then she said: 'Bring him in here.'

The domestic, who was on licence from the nearby mental hospital, went as near to dropping a curtsy as the usage of 1957 permitted, and then went out and brought Royston in.

Matron went on writing at her desk and did not look up at him. Royston at first stood quietly in the middle of the little office; then, as the silence prolonged itself, he began looking furtively and then openly round the room. Then he cleared his throat and blushed. Matron did not look up, but continued writing. It takes considerable willpower, when in the presence of another human being, to prolong a silence for one minute. Matron managed three. Then she put down her pen, blotted what she had written, and turned to look him up and down. As far as she was concerned, all the boys of this age played guitars and bashed up elderly shopkeepers. In the face of this, Royston's mouth went as dry as a warm towel. When he at last struggled to break this unnerving silence, the words would hardly come, but they were in fact the right ones: 'I'm very sorry to trouble you, madam –'

Not the faintest creak of a stay-bone betrayed that Matron was mollified, but somehow Royston felt encouraged to continue: 'I've come here looking for my mother.'

'Surely you know the visiting hours? Seven to eight.'

'Oh.' Then Royston dimly remembered visiting hours at the Remand Home. 'Oh, but my mother isn't here now!'

The Matron continued to stare at him in silence.

'You see,' floundered Royston, 'I was born here, that's a long time ago, and then I was adopted and then I – well, I sort of heard my real mother was dead, so I – so I – came to find out what she looked like.'

His voice tailed off into a miserable whisper; the story sounded feeble, even to him.

Matron continued to look at him in silence, but now she was slowly nodding her head. After a long pause she said: 'You were adopted, you say?'

'Yes.'

'As a tiny baby?'

'Well – yes.'

'Then as soon as that adoption order was made, your real mother, as I think you mistakenly call her, finished with you. You were no more concern of hers; she was no more concern of yours. She voluntarily gave her consent to the adoption, and after that she was finished.'

The edge of her hand descended on her desk like a butcher's cleaver.

'But I only wanted –'

'You should be grateful for what's been done for you, have you ever thought of that? You're alive and well, you're decently dressed, well-fed too, I expect, and who takes the credit for that? Your real mother. Not your natural mother, your real mother. My advice to you is to go home to her and think about that.'

'But I only thought –'

'Take my advice, young man: I know what I'm talking about. Go home to your real mother.'

Matron had put on her most steely look, but Royston summoned up every ounce of reserve strength and stood his ground and cried: 'But please, madam, please, tell me what sort of lady she was; her name was Hook.'

'Violet Hook.' There was an extraordinary mad glitter shining from behind those spectacles, but only for a moment. Then Matron said: 'Yes. She's dead. She's been dead to you since that adoption order was signed.'

She did not stand up, or point dramatically at the door, or even incline her head; but Royston shot out of the room without another word.

He went down the corridor towards the glossy entrance hall with its urn full of growing daffodils, and a humpy little woman with lascivious eyes and no teeth clutched his arm and said ''Allo!'

Royston trudged on. This was the domestic who had brought him into the place.

'Finished?'

He was embarrassed more by her obvious mental defect than her physical deformities; he looked away from her.

'I listened outside the door,' she said. 'You want to find Violet 'Ook, don't yer?'

Royston stopped dead. '*You* – know her?'

'My best friend, she is, Violet is. Mates, we are. 'Ow much will you give me to tell you where she is?'

'What – what –?'

'Come on, give us four bob for some fags.'

'Do you mean to say she's alive?'

'Come on, come on, four bob or Matron'll catch us, come on!'

'Where is she? *Where is she?*'

'Don't you 'urt me or I'll 'oller! Come on, come on, quick!'

Royston gave her his last five bob and she said: 'Two Chertsey Road.'

It was most peculiar, the room had suddenly become diagonal and then the corners stretched towards infinity, to infinity; and the floor laid itself against Royston's cheek. It was some time before he felt that the floor was cold, even longer before he found his cheek was bruised and swollen. . . .

'Yes, come in, Miss Mole: I think I've got some news, for what it's worth.'

'Oh sir, what?'

Mr Stokes told her.

'Oh, my dear lor. Yes, I 'spect that's him all right, whatever's he doing there?'

'He's been looking for his mother, Miss Mole, just as you thought he would one day.'

'But why Chipham?'

'He was adopted there, you see; I do know that, though I know precious little else.'

'How did he find that out?'

'He went back to the Beedmans, Miss Mole, and I feel quite sure that he got into their house while they were out and pinched all the adoption documents. I really can't understand why that woman kept them, feeling the way she did – I suppose she'd forgotten all about them. Anyway, Royston got them. He'd have discovered from them the name of his mother and I think her address; I'm not sure about that, but at least he'd have had something to go on, some clue about her.'

'But Mr Stokes, couldn't you have found it out too and headed him off, or caught him on the way?'

'No, for two reasons – three reasons if you count that I've been an absolute clot over this case. You see, I should have noted down the details of Royston's natural parents, but I didn't. So Royston got the adoption certificates with all the information, and Mrs Beedman couldn't remember any of it, she thought the mother was called Butcher or Baker, but I haven't been able to trace either of those names yet.'

'You know, beg pardon, Mr Stokes, but that Mrs Beedman just about infuriates me. You'd think she'd have been enough interested in the poor little kid to remember details about him.'

'I don't know, Miss Mole, perhaps she deliberately refused to remember that some other woman had done what she couldn't do. Oh no, I don't think she ever was really interested in Royston.'

'What was your other reason, Mr Stokes?'

'Well, it's a funny thing, but the people we deal with, our clients as we call them, seem to be able to do something that we can never do: they can seek each other out. It's as though, when you lift up the stone of conventional society, underneath there's a lot of little creatures going on in quite a strange way and all knowing each other. Royston's gone under the stone now. He in his position has got a better chance of finding his mum than I have in my position.'

Miss Mole sat silently considering this. Mr Stokes was slumped sideways in his chair, doodling on his blotter. He found Miss Mole very easy to confide in.

'Unless we have a big stroke of luck, I don't think I shall find the mother.'

'But Mr Stokes, don't we want to find Royston?'

'Oh yes, of course, but I want to find that mother first. You see, Miss Mole, this is what often happens – a young girl, in her teens, goes off the rails a bit and has a baby. She can't support it, so she places it for adoption. Quite often she steadies down afterwards and presently she marries. She finds she can't bring herself to tell her husband about the baby – perhaps she thinks she'll break up the marriage, probably she thinks the baby's over and done with, all buttoned up somewhere, why run risks for something that's all neatly disposed of? And time goes on, and the more time that passes the less she can possibly mention the baby. She has legitimate kids, and they grow up; and then, when those kids are nine or ten and everything's peaceful and going along nicely, suddenly in through the door walks – well, you can imagine!'

'Lord love us, Mr Stokes! But that's *terrible*!'

'It is terrible, Miss Mole; at least, it could be terrible. That's why, if I can't find Royston, I want to find the mother first. I might just be able to prepare her beforehand, or at least lie in wait for the boy outside.'

The telephone rang.

'Mr Stokes?' The voice was rich and fruity.

'Yes, speaking. Who is that?'

'Harris, P.O. Chipham. Just found a note on me desk askin' me to ring you, what's it all about?'

'Oh Mr Harris, how good of you to ring! Mr Harris, I want to try and trace the mother of a boy who was adopted some years ago – the adoption's since broken down and the boy is in our care – I'm wondering if your long memory can bring up any information that could help me?'

'Do me best, old boy. When was the Order made?'

'Late '42, I think, or early '43.'

'H'm. Before the Americans came – we had lots of adoptions afterwards. What was the name of the infant?'

'I'm not sure, Butcher, I'm told, or possibly Baker.'

'Butcher, Butcher, Baker, Gwendoline Baker. No, that was this year. Nothin' rings a bell, old boy, sorry.'

'During the war? About Alamein time? Does the name Beedman register at all?'

'Beedman, Beedman. There's a teeny tinkle there, old boy. Beedman, yes, weren't those the adopters?'

'Yes.'

'I remember, yes – he was a hatter or a tailor or somethin', wholesale tailor, that's it. Yes, Beedman! I recall: nice people, well-off, very well-meanin'.'

Stokes' eyelids blinked loudly, had he heard aright?

'What was the name of the child, Mr Harris?'

'Why, the Beedmans, didn't they have Vi Hook's baby? Yes, I'm sure they did. Don't remember the baby's first name, but Vi Hook was the mother. Yes, the Beedmans paid for her to go to that ghastly Nursing Home. That was it.'

'Mr Harris, have you any idea where I might find this Hook girl now?'

'What, Vi? Yes, old boy. She's still around, Vi is, see her meself occasionally round the town. Oh, yes, she's still extant, old Vi.'

'In Chipham?'

'Certainly in Chipham! She lives in Chertsey Road: on the corner of Green Lane, I forget if it's one or two, but you can't miss it. On the corner of Chertsey Road and Green Lane.'

'Mr Harris, I can't thank you enough.'

'You're welcome, old boy. Glad to help. Good huntin'!'

As Mr Stokes put down the telephone, he and Miss Mole let out their breath together.

'I'd better go over there straight away, Miss Mole, if you'll excuse me.'

'Mr Stokes, please, let me come with you?'

Stokes stopped in his tracks and looked at her. On the one hand, he had the feeling most social workers have of wanting to go it alone, of not liking somebody else watching him at work. And least of all an untrained foster-mother in a delicate situation like this! But on the other hand, there was warmth of sympathy between them. She and he seemed to be the only two people who really cared about Royston, this maddening kid who by any dispassionate standards was nothing but a damned nuisance, a delinquent, a fly-by-night, an ungrateful rogue, amoral, rebellious – and yet in trouble. And likely to be in more trouble.

'O.K., Miss Mole,' he said. 'Come on!'

Royston was running, bolting for it down Gisborne Hill, cupping his hurt cheek in his hand. When he had fainted, he had banged his elbow and his knee, and they throbbed; and he had left his bag behind; but he was away from there, he was away from that ogress in blue serge with her raking questions he was too confused to answer satisfactorily until at last she half turned her head to send a nurse to telephone for the police; and he had taken two long, sobbing breaths and then bolted for it and got away and gone running, running, down the hill and left and right in a maze of roads until the stitch in his side grew unbearable and he stopped with his breath whistling in his chest, and realized that all was quiet behind him.

For five minutes he sagged against a wall with his head down, gasping and swallowing for breath, until he had got himself under control; and then, still holding his cheek, and occasionally asking the way from passers-by, he set off pad-padding and turned into Chertsey Road.

He had come in from the wrong end. 100 – 98 – 96 – he slowed down to a steady walk. Not a bad sort of street. Council houses. Cars parked in the road under tarpaulins. The bluish flicker of the telly in darkened lounges. 74 – 72 – 70 – she'll be married, I expect, to a railwayman, a nice quiet fellow with a motor-bike and sidecar. I expect she'll be sitting by her telly with a cup of tea and her slippered feet on a pouffe. She won't half be surprised to see me! 38 – 36 – 34, Royston was walking very slowly. Very surprised. Angry surprise, perhaps. She might be cross – and – and say – well, so what? What did he care after all this time, huh, let her – and yet if only, if only she'd just look up and smile and – Royston came to a dead stop.

There was a light in the window of Number Two.

He stood in the shadow of the privet hedge at Number Four, and became aware of the smell of fried onions.

Then he crossed the road and looked at the house from the opposite pavement. He couldn't see in.

Well, let's go home now. I've found it, there it is. I can't go in; I couldn't possibly go in.

Home? Home?

He suddenly began to shiver all over and breathe quickly.

Then he looked very carefully to left and to right and marched across the road and in at the gate and knocked on the door.

There was a peculiar swishing sound from inside the house as though a wicker basket were being dragged over the floor, but before he could work out what it was, the door was crashed open six inches and a woman's voice said: 'Yes?'

'Mrs Hook?' quavered Royston.

'Mrs 'Ook, yes. Who's that, then?'

'Royston.'

'Oh, yes.'

There was a pause. A voice from within called: ''Oo is it, Nan?'

'Royston.'

'Oh,' said the voice indifferently.

The smell of fried onions was strong under the dark little porch. Royston was puzzled; the woman at the door looked bulky and sounded old. He gulped and said: 'Mrs Violet Hook?'

'Oh, you want Vi? Oh, you should 'ave said. I'm *Mrs* 'Ook, see. Vi! It's for you. Well, come in, my duck, no standin' on ceremony 'ere, eh? Don't want to be shy of us.'

Royston stepped forward into the dark passage, the uncarpeted stairs rising before him, and there was his mother peering at him out of the living-room.

She was a small, ferret-faced, ginger-haired woman with a cigarette stuck in the corner of her mouth. She held a baby over one shoulder and was mechanically patting its bottom. Overhead, on a cord, streaky vests and nappies crowded round the naked electric light bulb; a shaft of light shone on Violet's hair.

''Ow d'yer do,' she said.

'It's Royston come to see us,' said the old woman in a pleased voice. She was between him and the door; he edged reluctantly into the room. A small child with a ferret face and ginger hair ran forward and then grew shy and clutched at Vi's skirt.

'Say 'allo to Royston, then,' said the old woman. 'Come on, Elaine, where's your manners – ah, she's shy! Come on 'en, come to your Nana.'

Elaine buried her face in her mother's skirt, and Vi said in a puzzled voice: 'You wanted me, mate? Where yer come from, then, from work?'

Royston swallowed and said brusquely: 'You called me Christopher when you had me.'

'Did I?' said Vi indifferently. 'Nan! Turn the gas down a bit, will yer?'

'Christopher, you called me Christopher!'

Vi shifted the baby on to the other shoulder, dragged her cigarette from the lips it had stuck to, and said: 'Oh! Oh Chrissie! 'Im! Nan, it's Chrissie!'

'Oh yes? That's nice.'

'Don't you remember? The one wot we 'ad adopted, when we was up Cottonmill. You know.'

'Oh yes? Oh my word. Ain't he grown!' Nana grinned at him; her mouth was a black hole between two yellow fangs.

'Mum!' said a muffled voice.

'Shut up, Elaine, mummy's speaking.'

'Wanna lolly.'

'Belt up, Elaine, will you! Go and find Tracy, where is 'e? Tell 'im his big brother's come to see 'im, go on!'

But Elaine did not move.

'Oh 'im!' cried Nana. 'I din't realize! Oh there. You don't remember me, eh, your old Nana?'

Royston shook his head mutely. Suddenly tears began to roll slowly down his cheeks.

'Ah bless 'im, he's upset!' said Nana. ''Ere, you want a cup o' tea, comin' in out the cold like that. Sit down, I'll get yer a cup o' tea.' She got an enamel mug with dregs of tea in it, swished it round, threw the dregs on the fire, filled the mug with greenish tea from a blue enamel teapot, added condensed milk, put in three dessertspoonfuls of sugar, left the spoon in the mug, and put the mug on the edge of the table. 'There you are, my ducks, that's wot you need. That'll put new 'eart into yer.'

Royston began to sob bitterly. Elaine suddenly burst into a sympathetic howl. Vi cuffed her absent-mindedly and then gave her sixpence.

'Go on, then, go and get two lollies and give Tracy one and then come straight back 'ere and no messin' about on the way, mind!'

Vi turned back to Royston and said in a calculating voice: 'So you'll be fifteen now?'

'Ha!' said Nana. 'So 'e will! Fifteen! Fancy!'

Royston snivelled.

'I work at the Klaxon,' said Vi.

'Bin there a week now, your mummy has.'

'You 'ave to start low,' said Vi, 'but once you're on piece rates, well, some o' the boys I know knock up nine, ten a week.'

'Ha!' cried Nana triumphantly.

Suddenly Royston realized what this conversation was about. He jerked his head up like a startled deer. Vi was holding the cigarette to her lips and gazing at his clothes through narrow eyes. Nana was smiling wetly. The heavy fumes of frying fat moved in oily coils from the cooking-stove in the corner. The room began to swirl round Royston, become fluid, flow past him, carry him like a river onward and past those yellow fangs into Nana's mouth. . . .

With a frightful high cry, Royston wrenched himself backwards, along the passage, out through the broken-down door, down the muddy path between dismembered tricycles, and into the glorious street, where he drew one long sobbing breath and then began to fall towards the gutter.

Mr Stokes got him under one arm, and Miss Mole under the other.

16

'Now last of all there's this Hook creature,' said Miss Kelpie, smothering a yawn: this Case Conference had gone on too long already. 'Warden?'

'He's deteriorated since he was here before,' said Mr Lloyd-Chamberlain reluctantly. 'Not much more than a big lout now, I'm afraid; slops around, smokes, won't wash, dumb insolence; generally a thoroughly couldn't-care-less attitude.'

'Oh dear. Poor old Royston. Well, it's not to be wondered at. Doctor?'

The psychiatrist removed his large spectacles. 'This boy is definitely in depression at the moment,' he said. 'I think he's in a mild post-traumatic condition; mind you I stress that it's mild – I don't think he's heading for a psychosis or anything like that, but I'm not surprised to hear that he's difficult to live with in this phase, and probably rejecting all attempts to help him.'

'Cor, I'll say he is,' said the Senior Housemother.

Mr Ponto asked: 'Is he going down the drain, doctor?'

'I think he's very delicately balanced at the moment. I think with the wrong handling now, he might very well become anti-social. Not dangerously so, for he's a remarkably controlled child, considering the case history, and I wouldn't describe him yet as a delinquent.'

'But what about that money he stole from the B.B. hut and that lead-stealing, and that breaking and entering at the Beedmans?'

'I don't regard that as delinquency.'

'Well, what the hell else was it?' asked Mr Ponto, baffled.

'They were not hostile, revengeful or negativistic actions,' said Dr Maclaren. 'They formed a positive constructive part of his campaign to seek out his mother, which was, after all, a good thing to be doing. I'd like to say, Miss Kelpie, that I think you were very wise not to prosecute the boy for those offences: provided he makes restitution, of course.'

'He's doing that,' said Mr Lloyd-Chamberlain.

Mr Ponto said: 'But he didn't have to steal the money: he could have saved up, or got a paper-round and earned it, or he could have asked one of us to find his mother – I would very gladly have gone to Somerset House for him, but he never asked.'

Dr Maclaren ran an amused glance over Mr Ponto's tubby little figure, but made no answer.

Miss Kelpie asked: 'Isn't there the possibility that now he's found he can get lots of money quickly by crime, he'll do it again?'

'Not at the moment, I think,' said the psychiatrist. 'You see, the drive to get money at all costs is no longer there: he's found his mother at last and the fantasy-image has been exorcized. But if he runs into disappointment or rejection again, oh yes, I think he may well remember what he's learnt.'

Miss Kelpie said: 'It's clear, isn't it, that the whole problem is what we do with him now. He's fifteen, he's due to start work, he can't stop here at Banns Cross, and we shall evidently have to take care what we do. Doctor, will you start us off?'

'I think that the best placing for this boy will probably be a hostel. He needs a period of stability; he certainly doesn't wish to have to become involved in emotional relationships, as with foster-parents; he needs trained rather than intuitive help; and above all, he needs dependability, a secure footing under him.'

'But only for a period? You think he could be transferred to a foster-home later?'

'Oh, yes, that should be the ultimate aim, but not at this stage.'

'Right. Now, there are alternatives – residential employment, hotel work, or H.M. Forces.'

Mr Lloyd-Chamberlain said: 'I'd like to see this boy in the Navy: I think it would be the making of him, and I've broached the subject – delicately, of course. But he's simply not interested.'

'You can take a boy to the water, but you can't make him go on it,' said the Chief Welfare Officer.

'Quite. Now, what about a trade school – farming or that big place Barnardo's run?'

'That's a very excellent and useful establishment, Miss Kelpie, but I don't think it's right for this particular boy at this particular time. I think it's too big. I think *he* would feel that he'd simply been bunged away in another institution. I prefer the hostel.'

'Yes. Well, all right, then, it looks like a hostel for Royston.'

And then Mr Stokes, who had been sitting silently all afternoon through a lot of cases he was not concerned with, said: 'I don't agree.'

'Ha!' cried Miss Kelpie. 'Our strong, silent man. Yes, David, come in.'

Mr Stokes said: 'I'd just like first to put the negative aspect, the objections to hostel placement. Dr Maclaren has mentioned the boy's need for dependability and security, but at the rate that staff change in hostels, I can't see how he'll find it. Every few months in a hostel you've got to get used to new staff, new rules, new ideas – it's terribly unsettling.'

Miss Kelpie nodded encouragingly and Stokes went on: 'Secondly, Dr Maclaren says this boy is balanced on the brink of delinquency. You know the sort of chuck-out boys who get sent to hostels; Royston would have a strong pull exerted on him by the dishonest element – he might not be able to hold out against it. Finally, if it must be a hostel, the only one available to us at present is Bottingham Park; and in Bottingham Park is a youth named Archibald Tod.'

'Oh!' said Miss Kelpie. 'I didn't know Tod was there. Why?'

'Indecent assault on a little girl.'

'What were the details?' asked Mr Ponto.

'That's not relevant,' said Miss Kelpie. 'But it is relevant that Tod's there. He has a very bad influence on Royston, hasn't he, Warden?'

'Yes: while they were here before they went on the loose together.'

'I think that does it,' said Miss Kelpie. 'But what on earth else can you do, David? You want to risk him in lodgings?'

'I think,' said Stokes slowly, 'that a hostel is very useful for a boy who just can't tolerate personal relationships, the chap who gets knocked sideways by the very intimacy of the thing. But Royston doesn't strike me as a boy like that. I think he's one who is capable of making and responding to a good relationship; he always has been but the poor bloke's only experienced rotten ones.'

'But where are you going to get a good relationship in a short time?'

'From Miss Mole,' said Mr Stokes.

'A single woman?' asked Dr Maclaren sharply, and then looked very dubious.

'Oh you can't, David! You can't risk it. The boy's got to get used to changing from Home to foster-home and at the same time make the change from school to work, and there's no father-figure there and in any case I feel most dubious about an elderly spinster taking on responsibility for an adolescent youth.' Nobody reminded Miss Kelpie of her own position of responsibility.

'Nevertheless, I feel that Miss Mole has emerged as the one adult in this whole situation who cares about Royston as a person,' said Mr Stokes. 'She's stuck by him loyally for a year, she's seen him in various moods, she's a sensible and sensitive person, and she's the one element of goodness in this, whereas everything else you've suggested you must admit is nothing but an expedient.'

'But it's not even a good risk, David. It's not even a calculated risk – it's just a desperately unsafe gamble. I propose we put the boy in the hostel, preserve and build up the relationship with Miss Mole, and board him out with her in a year's time. By then he'll be used to employment, he'll be more mature in every way, he'll have had that control and training just when he needs them, and, well, in every way I feel that's the most sensible and safe compromise.'

But Mr Stokes went on obstinately shaking his head. 'It doesn't dispose of my objections to the hostel,' he said. 'Tod is there, whether we like it or not, and the staff position is shaky. And beyond that, I do feel that just at this stage, while Royston's on the rebound, he's in the mood to respond, he *wants* to respond, but he doesn't quite know what to. Give him a year in a hostel and either he'll respond to the wrong person or he'll lose the whole desire to respond – he'll get frosted off. This, here and now, is the golden moment.'

There was a long, uneasy silence. Miss Kelpie eventually raised her head. 'Heaven forbid that I should ever decide a child's future by a committee vote,' she said, 'but I would be most interested to know the feeling of the meeting. How many feel that this boy should go to the hostel?'

Five of the ten people present raised their hands, and after a quick look round, Mr Ponto raised his, too.

'Six to three, David; and I'm inclined to the hostel idea myself, so that's seven to three.' Miss Kelpie shook her head and pursed her lips.

And then Dr Maclaren spoke. 'One moment. Excuse me, Miss Kelpie. Stokes: when that boy rushed out of his mother's house and took a nose-dive into the gutter, you and Miss Mole caught hold of him, didn't you?'

'Yes.'

'What were the boy's first words after that?'

Mr Stokes thought hard, and replied: 'He said "Thanks, Auntie".'

The psychiatrist smiled all over his jolly red face. 'I withdraw,' he said. 'I withdraw my hostel, and I'll not object to boarding out with Miss Mole. But you know, Stokes, you're running one hell of a risk. This boy was rejected by his own mother, then rejected by his adoptive mother, and then experienced what were virtually two more rejections, by his own mother again and by the Woodingtons. If this foster-mother fails him – and she's likely to have the devil of a time with him – then you can look out for real trouble.'

Mr Stokes nodded. 'Nevertheless,' he said. 'I'd always prefer to let a little bird out of its cage and risk the cat catching it.'

Miss Mole was overjoyed when she heard about the decision: she wanted to 'make up to poor Roy for all he's been through'. But Mr Stokes drove down twice for long conferences with her, and sufficiently schooled her so that when Royston finally arrived with his new suitcase she was warm and pleasant and she provided eggs and chips for tea, but she didn't clasp him to her bosom. She yearned to treat him as a little boy, but steadfastly she treated him as an adult.

She let him mooch about idly for a few days; sometimes she went with him, sometimes not. She had television now, and in the evenings they would sit engrossed by the quiz shows on I.T.V., willing the contestants towards the right box, or discussing afterwards whether they would have taken the cash or the car.

Royston went by himself to the Youth Employment Office, but Miss Mole knew that Mr Stokes had been ahead to trample down the undergrowth. Indeed, Royston had a most sympathetic interview and was given a card of introduction to an employer. He came home during the afternoon.

'Did you get the job, Roy?'

'Yes!' he said, grinning delightedly; then he remembered that he was the hard-done-by-Hook, and he added: 'Blooming old dump, and only three quid a week.'

'Ah, well, it'll put some money in your pocket, and keep you going till something better turns up,' said Miss Mole philosophically.

However, she noticed that for the next few days he went whistling merrily around the house; and during his first week he went off in the mornings, and returned in the evenings, so cheerily that she felt sure all was well.

Mr Stokes advised her that Royston's contribution for board and lodging would be twenty-six shillings.

'Oh, I couldn't take the money, Mr Stokes. You know I never took him for what I could get out of him.'

'It's the principle of the thing, Miss Mole: he's got to learn the value of money by allocating so much for clothes, so much for fares, so much for insurance, and so much for board and lodging.'

'But it's going to spoil everything, if money starts coming between us; makes me out no more than a landlady.'

'It won't, Miss Mole. Royston knows that all the boys in care do the same; he knows it's the system. Besides, you know, it often helps these boys to feel they're really a useful part of the household.'

Miss Mole consented dubiously, but later she had to admit that Royston accepted the position without apparent rancour.

September – October – November.

'I think he's going to be all right, Mr Stokes. He loves his job; never any trouble to get him off in the mornings; and from little bits he comes out with I know he's happy there.'

'What about his leisure time?'

'Well, we've got a sort of routine. Fridays, when he's paid, he goes to the pictures. Saturdays, I take him out somewhere. Sundays we stop in for "What's My Line"; Mondays we stop in, too. Tuesdays he'll go to his Youth Club. Wednesdays I go to a whist drive and sometimes he'll come too, sometimes he'll stop at home. Thursdays he's always in, he's usually skint by then, Poor old Roy, ten bob pocket-money doesn't go far these days.'

'You make him stick to it?'

'Well, I see he's not short of a cigarette; otherwise he has to manage on it, yes.'

'What's he like in himself, Miss Mole? Does he still get these dark moods?'

'Oh, he's all right reelly, old Roy is. A bit gruff sometimes. It seems to me, Mr Stokes, that every now and then he's got to remind himself that he's an unwanted child, that he's not supposed to be having a good time. Then, yes, I will admit he has his moments. But I leave him alone, he'll come round in his own good time. Don't get me wrong, Mr Stokes, he's reelly a good boy; remembered my birthday, he brought me that.' She nodded towards an emaciated plaster seagull which was swooping tiredly on the wall.

They were away for Christmas; Miss Mole decided to do something that was new to both of them, and they went for a 'traditional Yuletide' in a hotel up north. It turned out to be opulent but not very comfortable.

It was after Christmas that the trouble started.

'I don't know what's come over the boy, Mr Stokes; honestly, I'm at my wits' end.'

'What's he actually doing?'

'It's not so much what he does – it's more his manner. I don't know, he's suddenly got just thoroughly awkward. He won't wash, goes off in the morning just as he is, and in the evenings sits down for his tea covered with that grease and stuff from work. And if I tell him, I get such a look! If looks could kill, Mr Stokes!'

Mr Stokes clucked sympathetically. He looked worried.

'And last Sunday, that nearly finished me: lay abed, he did, till three o'clock in the afternoon. I hotted his breakfast up twice, but no, and what to do about dinner I didn't know. Come three o'clock, down comes his lordship, says he isn't hungry and flings off out and I see no more of him till half past ten that night! Well, where's the boy been, Mr Stokes? He can't have been up to any good, all that time, and I was worried stiff – I mean, you hear such stories.'

'Any trouble over money?'

'No, I must say he's very good that way, hands over his bit every Friday and no trouble. I just don't understand him, Mr Stokes, what's got into the boy?'

'He might be testing you out. I've seen this in younger boys – they suddenly start playing up to see if their foster-mothers will still love them even if they're naughty.'

'Well, maybe, but what do I *do* about it? It's all very well you saying let him go his own way, but you can't stand back and watch a decent lad like that go to the dogs and not *do* anything. And yet if I talk to him it only makes things worse.'

'I know it's terribly difficult, Miss Mole. He's at the rebellious age, and these teenagers have got to have something to rebel against or they're lost. And yet on the other hand, with a boy of Royston's background, if you lay down the law too hard you may drive him over the brink. The only thing I can suggest is that you take the thing that really worries you most and concentrate on trying to put that right. Otherwise you'll just find yourself nag, nag, nagging all the time.'

'Mr Stokes, has he got in with that Tod boy again?'

'Not to my knowledge, Miss Mole; I think this is something inside Royston himself.'

'I wish I knew what it was. But you will talk to him, Mr Stokes?'

'Oh, yes: I'll get hold of him after work.'

'I hope you'll get somewhere with him, get him to see a bit of sense. I'm reelly terribly worried.'

Miss Mole was, in fact, not far from tears, and when he drove home that night Mr Stokes was also feeling despondent. He had spent a long hour with a smouldering Royston, a Royston who, when tackled about his misdemeanours, had barely kept within the civilities. Mr Stokes felt he had been wrestling with the Devil. And yet, even so, there had been more than a gleam of remorse when the boy had been told that he was upsetting Miss Mole. There was still that thread of good feeling, and there was still hope if the boy could get free of this black undertow that gripped him. Mr Stokes thought wearily that the boy would hold steady for another week and if a visit could be fitted in every week after that without fail, he, Stokes, might just manage to hang on to the lad.

Six days later Miss Mole telephoned.

'Mr Stokes, Royston's on the loose again.'

'*What!*'

'Packed in his job, come back here and took all his clothes, and vanished. This was last night.'

'I'll come straight over, Miss Mole.'

'Well, I'd like to see *you*, Mr Stokes; but I don't know if I ever want to see that boy again.'

17

Mr Stokes drove over to East Whixham in forty-five minutes, which was a hair-raising time for that journey.

'My word, you've been quick!' said Miss Mole. 'I'll put the kettle on.'

'Don't make tea just for me, Miss Mole.'

'No, no, I've been waiting for you to come so's I could have some myself. I didn't sleep too well last night, matter of fact.'

No, she looked a bit rough, thought Mr Stokes, poor old soul. Stray locks of hair had been allowed to escape from their braids, and her eyes were not their usual sharp blue.

When they were sipping their tea, Mr Stokes said: 'Now, supposing you tell me all about it, Miss Mole?'

'I can't tell you much more than I already have. I rang the works; the manager was very nice, he said they were sorry to lose Roy, but he'd given in his notice in the proper way and said he'd got another job to go to, so, of course, they didn't suspect anything. He'd actually given in his notice before you saw him last week.'

'I see.'

'I spoke a bit about why I was worried, and the man said he was sorry and that if ever Roy wanted to change his mind, they'd be pleased to have him back there, because he was a cheerful and willing lad. Those were his very words.'

'Well, that's something, I suppose. They couldn't give you any clue as to why this suddenly blew up like this?'

'No. They did say they thought that Royston went off with another boy after work last evening.'

'What sort of a boy?'

'I don't know. Nobody reelly bothered to notice. Mr Stokes, he's not in with that Tod again, is he?'

'Well, not up until Monday, Miss Mole. I rang the hostel, as you were worried, and Tod was still there then, and going along, you know, reasonably. Anyway, after that Royston came home and fetched his clothes?'

'Yes. He knew I'd be out: I was having tea with Lily Spence, from the shop. He took everything of his that was in this house, barring that blooming seagull, and how I hate the sight of that up there leering at me!'

Miss Mole's eyes had become very bright, but unfortunately Mr Stokes did not notice. 'How had Royston been during the week since I was down?' he asked.

'Rotten! No, he wasn't rotten, but the week was. Never did a thing wrong and all the time it seemed as though he was doing the right things because he'd been ordered to, not because he wanted to please me. With a bad grace. Mr Stokes, I've been so unhappy –'

Miss Mole's chin suddenly wobbled, she gulped, and then burst into a cascade of sobs; snivelled, 'Excuse me,' and walked quickly out of the room. Mr Stokes didn't know where to look, and his hands felt too large.

Presently she came back and resumed her seat with a sigh. 'Would you pour me out another cup of tea, my dear?' she said. 'I feel better now. I've been wanting to do that for a long time. I'm sorry it was when you were here, though.'

'That's O.K., Miss Mole. Here you are. Don't you worry so much. You let me do the worrying – that's what I'm paid for.'

'It's not so easy as that, Mr Stokes. You know, I told you on the telephone that I never wanted to see Roy again. I don't know what made me say that, but it wasn't true – I'd give my right arm to see him again. But I don't know, after all this, whether I ought to have him back.'

'Well, I've got every confidence in you, Miss Mole.'

'It's not that. Thanks all the same. It's just that I feel I must be doing something badly wrong or he wouldn't have gone off like that.'

'I can't think that you are, Miss Mole, but I find it difficult to be convincing because frankly I haven't a clue as to why he has gone. The one thing I am sure about is that if this boy turns to us again, we mustn't let him down. You say you would have him back if he came to you?'

'Yes, if *he* comes. Like a shot I would, if he came of his own free will. But not if you just send him, Mr Stokes, or come with him. That won't do.'

'Well, it may not be easy for him. It would take a good deal of courage, even in an adult, to come back and face someone you've done this to.'

'Yes, I see that, but all the same I shan't be certain in my own mind that I mean anything to him unless he comes back of his own free will. And unless I'm certain, it's not much good me going on.'

'Miss Mole, is there some difficulty between you that's upsetting you, perhaps without your knowing? You know, unconsciously? Is it the money, or the extra work?'

'It's not the money, Mr Stokes, you know that. And the extra work's nothing – I've worked hard all my life and I like doing it. I know he brings mud and smell into the house and there's clearing up behind him and seeing to his washing and that, but that's woman's work, Mr Stokes; that's the nature of things, and I'm glad to be doing woman's work for a change. No: what gets me down is when I've put before him everything I stand for, shown him, without rubbing it in, everything my mum and dad showed me, he turns round and, if you'll pardon the expression, he just spits it all back in my face!'

'Ah!'

'Well, dear God, I've got to try, haven't I? You can't say I'm wrong because I believe in common decency?'

'No, of course you're not wrong, Miss Mole. It was just that I was wondering if – oh well, it doesn't help us now, anyway; we've got to find him first. I don't know what he thinks he's doing.'

'Has he turned back to crime, Mr Stokes?'

'Maybe. I wish to God I knew where he was.'

'All right 'ere, innit?' said Tod.

'Yes. Quite clean,' said Royston, slightly surprised.

'We'll be all right 'ere the night. There's an ole Scotchman down the end there, 'e's gorn down the boozer now, 'e won't trouble us.'

'What is this place, Tod?'

'Oh daft! Transport caff.'

'I know it's a transport caff,' said Royston irritably, 'but what's this place for? Staff?'

'Cor, some people ain't got no sense, 'ave they? Long-distance lorry drivers, you crumb! They gotta sleep somewhere, ain't they? Like ole Mac down there, 'e came from Glasgow, sleeps 'ere tonight, goes back tomorrow. As a matter of fack, 'e's a friend of mine, ole Mac is; going to teach me to drive, ole Mac is. I 'ad a look over 'is lorry, nuffing worth taking.' Tod took a deep drag on his cigarette and attempted to blow a smoke ring.

'How did you come to know about this place, Tod?'

'Oh, I know all the places. You know, going up an' down like I do, knowin' all the toffs, you get to know the places. It's one-and-six a night. You got any lolly?'

'I've got my wages.'

'Go 'alves, then.'

'What do you mean, go halves?'

'We're mates, ain't we?'

'Well – yes.'

'Well, then!'

'But, blimey, Tod, I earned it!'

'Muck your rotten luck, then. Oh all right: it's in yer wallet, I s'pose?'

'Never you mind!'

'Leave it in yer wallet, then; that'll be quite safe there when we go to sleep.'

Royston, whose cheeks had bright spots of anger in them, shifted crossly on his low stretcher bed and lit another cigarette. Tod was whistling tunelessly between his teeth. It was about nine o'clock and the evening seemed interminable.

'Tod.'

'Yer?'

'How did you come to be in East Whixham?'

'Come down for the dog meeting. I reg'ly patronize the dogs. Did very well too, made a thousand.'

'A thousand *quid*?'

'Yeah. Often do. You know the toffs, see, get to know the ploys, then yer quids in.'

'Well, go halves, then!'

Tod's eyes glittered suddenly. ''Fraid it ain't possible, old man,' he said. 'Sorry. I put it straight in the bank, see. I 'ave an account now, now I'm in the big time – Bank of England, of course. Well, it's bettern' carryin' it round wiv yer, I mean you never know who's about, these days, do yer?'

(Tod had, in fact, spent the afternoon in the Pier Amusement Arcade, and had lost fourpence.)

'I don't get you, Tod,' said Royston. 'You're supposed to have all this money, but you don't seem to spend much of it on clothes.' Tod was wearing a black windcheater and tight, pale-blue jeans.

'What? Don't make me laugh! I got plenty o' clothes, lovely clothes, all the yobs turn to me for advice. Course. Stands to reason. But I don't cart 'em round wiv me, get in me way. We shall 'ave to flog yours.'

'Flog 'em?'

'Course. Don't want to be cluttered up wiv that ole junk. You ditch it tomorrer; be like me, dress unobstructively and don't cart nuffin' around. I only wear this junk 'cos it's more professional, like.'

'Are you on the loose from the hostel, Tod?'

'Hah! Not 'arf. Finished with that dump, mate. What? Stop in a muckin' ole dump like that? Hah; I finished with that place. Finished with the bleedin' Council, too. Come 'ere, go there, be a good boy! Phoo!'

'Won't they come after you, Tod?'

'No bloody fear, mate. I thrown 'em off the scent. I mean, I don't want to boast, but I'm pretty clever. Well, I should say, without boasting, very clever. See, I dropped the word, 'ere an' there, that I was going to Folkestone. Hah, hah! See their blooming ole faces when they look all round Folkestone an' I ain't there! Laugh! Cor! Anyway, see, they'll never think o' lookin' in Bottingham Hill.'

'Bottingham Hill? You going back there?'

'Course! You're comin' too.'

'But – can't we stop here?'

'No! You crummy dope! This is only for the night! Now, listen, Roy, I got it all figured, see, this is big, see. There's a geezer in Bottingham wot I know, 'e's a mate o' mine, matter of fack, wot I met up the billiard 'all. Fifteen, see; 'e's a butcher-boy. Now, every Sat'day – I got all this taped, see, I told yer I use me loaf, I'm pretty good at that – well, very good – every Sat'day 'e 'as to bring down the money wot they've took in the shop and put it in the bank.'

'Oh, blimey, Tod, we're not going to do a bank?'

'No, Gawd! Beedman, you ain't 'arf dozy. We're goin' to do the geezer.'

'Do him?'

'Yeah, course. You cosh 'im, see, jus' one good smack cross the back of 'is neck, it's easy, see. Then I grabs the bag an' we scarpers in different directions, see, then they can't foller us.'

'How much is in the bag?'

'Few 'undred.'

Royston considered. 'Why don't *you* cosh him?' he asked.

Tod evidently wasn't quite ready for this one. 'Well,' he said, and attempted to blow another smoke ring. 'Well-er-see, I ought to, I freely admit it. I'd be very good at it, better'n you anyway, only-er-well, the one wot does the coshin' 'as got to come very close, see, an' this geezer knowin' me, me bein' 'is mate, like, well 'e'd instantly reckernize me. No, you do the coshin', Roy, and then soon's 'e's out I'll be ready to Play my Part.'

Royston brooded on this with his eyes half closed, trying to visualize the scene. There was something savagely exciting about gripping the cosh, hardening one's jaw as one lifted up the weapon and glided forward and then – no. Somehow Royston couldn't visualize the next bit. Smashing into a pillow, yes, the edge of a table, yes. But the back of someone's neck? Oh well; for a few hundred pounds – here, wait a minute, what was this about running different ways?

'Tod.'

'Yer?'

'What happens after?'

'We go up West.'

'Where to?'

' 'Otel, prob'ly. Paddington, prob'ly. I know Paddington *very* well, I got loads o' mates in Paddington.'

'Then what?'

'Oh blimey, Beedman, you don't arf moan! 'Ow the 'ell should I know? 'Ave a shifty round Paddington, prob'ly, p'raps do a job there, then move on.'

'Move again?'

'Course! You gotta keep movin', that's the answer, see. They always looks for yer where yer hang out, so if yer not there they can't nick yer. Keep movin', see, and never make no statement, they can't get yer if yer don't make no statement, I know that.'

'And what do we do with the money?'

'Oh gawd, wot do you usually do wiv money? Spend it! Think of it. 'Undreds o' pounds.'

'Yes.'

'Couple 'undred nicker apiece for a minute's work – less'n that, 'arf a minute's work, ten seconds.'

'Yes.'

'An' after that – *enjoyment*!'

'I don't know.'

'Wot's the matter – you windy?'

Royston didn't reply.

'Gah! You're yeller. You're too dead flippin' windy to do anything. Even for a 'undred nicker.'

'It isn't that! Only what's the good of a hundred quid if we've got to go on the loose for the rest of our lives?'

'Wot's the good of life if you ain't on the loose? Blimey, Beedman, you want to creep back in a cage like a bleedin' budgie, you do! Sweat yer guts out for someone else, then 'and all yer lolly over to someone to look after yer, no thank you! 'Ere: you ain't supposin' that that ole girl o' yours *wants* yer, are yer?'

Royston was silent.

'Cos take it from me, mate, she only wants yer money.'

'She does not! She's got plenty of her own.'

'Then if she don't want money, she wants a little bit o' comfort now'n again.'

'No! Certainly not!'

'Ah, come orf it, Beedman –'

'And stop calling me Beedman!'

'Why, that's yer name, innit? Beedy Beedman? Weedy Beedy?'

'Shut your great fat gob!'

Tod was silent only for a moment. Then he said: 'Well? Are yer comin' in or not?'

'I don't know!' snarled Royston. 'I'm going to bed. I'll tell you in the morning.'

In the most gentle and imploring tone Royston had ever heard him use, Tod said: 'Don't give in to 'em, Roy. Don't leave it all to me.'

In silence Royston hung his jacket at the end of his bed, folded his trousers neatly and put them under the mattress, and crept into bed in his shirt and pants. Tod merely removed his shoes and flung himself down.

After the light was out Tod interrupted Royston's agonized indecision with a harsh whisper: 'Roy?'

'What now?'

'This ole girl o' yours – she's got money?'

'A bit.'

'And she's gettin' on a bit?'

'M'm.'

'An' she lives all alone?'

''Cept for me.'

'Cor! Where's she live?'

'I'm not going to tell you.'

'All right, I know, Kendal Rise, you told me once.'

There was a long pause. 'There's nuffin' to beat doin' up a woman, Roy! Nuffin'. It's – *agony*!'

Royston lay stiff and alert, listening to the rustle and gasp from Tod's bed, drowsily watching the square of skylight, hearing the occasional car whang down the main road outside. Then he fell asleep.

Suddenly he jerked awake and remembered just in time not to stop his even breathing. Under drooping eyelids he could just make out Tod standing and going through the pockets of the jacket at the end of the bed. Presently Tod gave a grunt, took something out, went over to his own bed and fiddled with his shoes, and then rolled under his blankets and was soon asleep.

Royston slept fitfully, waking every half-hour or so in a blurred panic, forcing himself each time to find out if he was awake or asleep. Several times in his dreams he became acutely aware that somebody elderly and kind was bending over him, and when he awoke he was genuinely puzzled because she was not there.

At the first sign that the skylight had gone a paler grey, he got up and silently dressed. Then he got Tod's shoes, and wedged in between the tongue and the upper he found his own three pounds. Carrying his shoes and his bag, he took himself out of the dormitory, flitted across the sodden cinders of the lorry-park, and started off through the morning mists on the long, long trudge back to Whixham.

He came up Kendal Rise only seconds after Mr Stokes's car had gone off round the bend; indeed, when he rang, Miss Mole thought it was Mr Stokes returning for something he had forgotten, and she jerked open the door with an amused smile.

The smile froze on her face, and she gave Royston a long, level stare.

Royston stared back at her in silence. Then he attempted to clear his throat, and then worked his jaw from side to side, and then at last in a queer little croak he said: 'Lo.'

Miss Mole opened the door wider and stood aside to let him enter.

As he crossed the threshold, her first words to him were: 'Oh, my dear lor, now just look at those trousers! Get yourself upstairs and change and I'll see if I can draw the edges together. Men!'

Royston went upstairs grinning all over his face.

It was a long time after – after she'd boiled up the milk for the coffee, after he'd fetched the coke in, after they'd heard

'Mrs Dale's Diary', in fact while she was peeling the potatoes for chips for dinner – that the doorbell rang.

'All right, Mum, I'll go,' said Royston, and opened the door. It was Tod.

He was standing with a comb in one hand, and while he looked at Royston he was running his thumb down the teeth of the comb with a whining ping.

Royston took a pace forward and with all his weight belted Tod full on the nose and laid him out flat among the London Pride.